PROTECTING YOU

A SMALL TOWN ROMANCE

BAILEY BROTHERS
BOOK 1

CLAIRE KINGSLEY

Always Have LLC

Published by Always Have, LLC

Edited by Elayne Morgan

Cover design by Lori Jackson

Cover photography by Wander Aguiar Photography

Cover model: Andrew Biernat

ISBN: 9798645749958

www.clairekingsleybooks.com

❀ Created with Vellum

For all my readers. Your love, support, and excitement for this series means everything.

ABOUT THIS BOOK

One night brings them together. Another night tears them apart.

Grace Miles misses her easy friendship with Asher, but growing up means growing apart. And really, how could he fall for her when they spent their childhood getting muddy in the creek and splitting sticks of gum?

But this summer, something feels different. If Grace didn't know better, she'd think Asher was flirting with her. Those dark eyes, hard body, and wicked smile make her insides swirl and her heart dare to hope for things she's convinced herself she'll never have.

Falling for your best friend shouldn't be complicated, but for Asher Bailey, loving Grace is anything but simple. The road to romance isn't smooth thanks to his pack of wild brothers who are protective of the girl next door, a take-no-sass grandmother, a small town where gossip is a spectator sport, and a feud that spans generations.

But Asher realizes his feelings are too big to ignore. Loving her isn't the risk. Losing her would be.

And one night, one kiss, changes everything.

Finally admitting their feelings is the beginning of their happily ever after. Until their fairy tale love story is tragically interrupted, and neither of them will ever be the same.

Author's note: Lifelong soulmates, ridiculous pranks, brother shenanigans, and a feuding town. Protecting You is the Bailey Brothers series origin story. Be there when it begins and fall in love with this wild band of unruly brothers. The series is meant to be read in order, and Grace and Asher's story concludes in Fighting for Us.

1

ASHER

Age 11

I startled at the sharp sound of grown-ups yelling. Dropping my stick in the trickling creek water, I whipped around to look, but my brothers were the only ones around. Evan was in a tree, probably trying to get away from the twins. Levi and Logan splashed downstream from me with Gavin, who was covered head to toe in mud.

Someone yelled again—a man's voice, loud and booming—and my stomach twisted. I didn't know why, but even if they weren't yelling at me, the sound of grown-ups fighting always gave me a stomachache.

Gram and Grandad never yelled, especially not at each other. Which meant it had to be Grace's mom, Miss Naomi, and her dad, Mr. Miles.

Grace's dad didn't live with them like some dads did, but he came to visit sometimes. I hated it when he came over. Not because it meant Grace would be busy and couldn't come outside with me, although I hated that too. She was my best friend and we saw each other every day, except when her dad was visiting.

The problem was, everyone got upset when Mr. Miles was here. Once I heard Gram say he always left messes behind. I used to think she meant he didn't clean up his dishes, but now I wondered if she meant a different kind of mess. A grown-up mess.

The yelling didn't stop, the loud voices carrying all the way down to the creek. I hopped over the shallow water and ran up the slope toward Grace's house. If this was making *my* stomach hurt, she was probably really upset.

I needed to find her.

It sounded like her parents were out front, so I raced across the grass. Gram was working in the garden, but she didn't call for me as I ran by and veered toward the space between our two houses.

Grace wasn't in her backyard, and I didn't see her on the side of the yard that faced our house. I slowed to a walk and carefully crept toward the front. I peeked onto their front porch but didn't see her there either.

Then I felt dumb. Of course she wasn't sitting on the porch while her parents yelled at each other.

She'd be hiding.

We had a lot of good hiding places. Gavin found the best ones, but he was also the smallest and could probably fit into a snake hole if he tried. Most of our favorite spots weren't near our houses. They were out on Gram and Grandad's land, past the gardens.

I hoped Grace had run down the hill and jumped the creek. Maybe she was waiting it out in a tree, or had gone out to the spot she called the fairy garden where she couldn't hear her parents fighting.

But I'd been playing at the creek all morning—bored

without her—and I hadn't seen her. If she were upset and wanted to hide out there, she'd have come to get me first.

Which meant she was hiding around here. Watching. Listening to them fight.

It made my stomach hurt worse.

I glared at Mr. Miles from behind the cover of a bush. Why did he have to shout so much? He was a big man, tall and always dressed like grown-ups on TV shows. His shirts weren't flannel like Grandad wore, but they had buttons, and sometimes he wore a tie.

I hated him. I hated his loud voice and his fancy car. But mostly I hated that every time he came to visit, something would make Grace cry.

Avoiding the front of the house so they wouldn't see me, I cut around back. Grace wasn't between the bushes and her house. She hadn't wedged herself into the space beneath the back steps.

There wasn't anywhere to hide on the other side of the house. I looked, but I didn't see her there either. Which meant she was probably inside.

The yelling continued, and I figured you could hear it inside even with all the windows shut. I ran around to the other side of the house and hunted for a few pebbles. Looking up at Grace's bedroom window, I tossed one of the small rocks at the glass.

It clicked when it hit, and I waited. But she didn't come. I tried again, but nothing happened. Maybe she wasn't in her room.

Dropping the last pebble, I ran to the back door. It was unlocked, like always, so I went in. She wasn't watching TV or having a snack in the kitchen. I raced up the stairs, my stomachache getting worse by the second.

Her bedroom door was open a crack, so I peeked inside. "Grace?"

A big lump under her covers moved.

"Gracie Bear, what are you doing?" I went in and lifted the edge of the covers so I could see underneath.

She was curled up with her arms grasping her knees. Her eyes were red, her cheeks streaked with tears.

It made me want to punch something.

"Can I come in your blanket fort?"

She sniffed. "It's not a good fort."

"Do you want to build a better one?"

She shook her head.

It made me so angry when she looked sad.

I lifted her comforter and crawled inside. She scooted over to make room as the blanket settled over the top of us. The air was warm under here, but it smelled good. Like laundry soap.

"My mom's mad at my dad," she said, her voice small.

"Yeah. Do you know why?"

"He was supposed to take me to Seattle to go to the big zoo. Now he says he can't." She sniffed. "Have you ever been to that zoo?"

"No."

"Me neither. Mom said there are zebras and giraffes and gorillas. And you can watch penguins swim in a pool."

I thought for a second. "Well, if your dad can't take you, I will. It's only five years until I can drive. I bet Grandad will let me borrow the truck and we'll go, just you and me."

She smiled a little. That made me feel better. And made me want to make her smile more.

I dug in my pocket, wondering if I had anything left from our last trip to the Sugar Shack for snacks. My fingers found a few empty wrappers, but I still had one stick of gum.

"Here." I held it out to her. "It's my last piece. Want it?"

She smiled again and took it. "Thanks. Let's split it."

Without waiting for me to answer, she opened the gum and ripped the pink strip in half. She handed one side to me and popped the other in her mouth.

Gum could fix a lot of things.

The air beneath the comforter was getting hot and stifling with two of us under here. I tossed it aside and hopped off the bed.

"Come on. Let's go."

She sat up and wiped her eyes. "Where?"

"Outside."

I reached for her hand and helped her slide off the bed. Smacking our gum, we ran downstairs and out the back door.

Her dad's voice boomed out front and she flinched. My first thought was to get her away from the arguing, but he made me so mad. He was supposed to take her to the zoo, and instead he'd made her cry. He was such a dumb jerk.

I grabbed her hand and led her around the side of the house, heading for the front.

"Where are we going?" she whispered.

"I have an idea."

We stopped next to the porch and crouched low so they couldn't see us. Miss Naomi had her hands on her hips and she looked mad. Scary mad. It wasn't good when Grace's mom made that face. It meant you were in big trouble.

Her dad had his back to us and his arms were crossed. But more importantly, his car was parked close by.

I took the gum out of my mouth and held out my hand. "Give me your gum."

"But it still has flavor."

I grinned. "Trust me. I have an idea."

As if she could read my mind—and sometimes I figured she could—she smiled back and handed me her chewed-up gum. "Do it."

I mushed our two pieces of gum together and watched Miss Naomi. I'd have to make a run for it and hope she didn't see me.

"Don't get caught," Grace whispered.

"I won't. But if I do, just run. I won't tell them you were here."

Staying low, I darted toward the car. The grown-ups kept arguing. I stretched the sticky wad of gum so it would cover more area and stuck it to the driver's side door handle, right where he'd grab it.

Grace clapped her hand over her mouth to keep from giggling out loud as I ran back to her.

"Let's go."

Grabbing each other's hands, we made a run for it, dashing for the creek. By the time we splashed through the water, Grace wasn't crying anymore. Her blond hair streamed behind her and she smiled big.

She made me feel kind of funny when she did that.

We kept going until the sound of her parents fighting faded behind us. Narrow pine trees replaced the grass and gardens that grew in our yards, their needles covering the ground. This was still our territory, although we had to be careful not to go too far. There were bears in the hills, and coyotes and who knew what else. I was pretty sure I could keep a coyote from hurting Grace, but I didn't want to come face to face with a bear.

Plus, if we couldn't hear Gram calling us in for dinner,

we'd get in trouble. I was already going to get it for the gum on Mr. Miles' car, but I didn't care. It was worth it.

We stopped when we got to a tall maple. It was a great climbing tree. Grace went up first, nimbly scaling the low branches. She was the best tree climber in Tilikum. She wasn't scared to go up really high. That wasn't the main reason she was my best friend, but it was one of them.

I followed and scooted out onto a thick branch to sit beside her. I had a fresh scrape on my leg, probably from the bark, but it wasn't bleeding and it only stung a little, so I ignored it.

Our legs dangled high above the ground. It felt like nothing could get us up here. Nothing could hurt us. It was me and Grace against the world.

Without saying anything, she leaned her head on my shoulder and grabbed my hand. I rested my head on top of hers. I liked it when she did this. It gave me a funny feeling in my stomach, like when she smiled really big, but it was a good feeling, not a bad one.

I wished I had more gum to give her, but I didn't. So I just sat with her, swinging my legs and holding her hand.

2

ASHER

Age 21

I stood looking out the upstairs window, like a puppy who'd just caught sight of his owner. Craning my neck to see, my face close to the glass. I hadn't come upstairs intending to stand here with my hands on the window frame, leaning so I could get a better view of my neighbor's house. Although now that I was up here, I couldn't remember why I'd come in the first place.

Grace was home for the summer.

My lip twitched in an almost-smile as I watched her get out of her beat-up Toyota Corolla. Her blond hair was in a ponytail and she wore a loose t-shirt and cut-offs, a pair of flip-flops on her feet. She paused outside her car, her hands on the open door, and looked around, like she was taking it all in.

Our houses sat at the end of a private drive, the narrow road bumpy with potholes. Her mom's house was newer than ours, but you wouldn't know by looking at it. The front porch was a patchwork of reclaimed wood my brothers and I had used to shore it up, and the whole thing needed a fresh coat of paint. The yard was tidy, mostly because Gram treated it like an extension of her gardens. Flowers bloomed in window boxes, and my brothers and I took care of mowing the lawn. But the whole place still looked tired and worn.

What was Grace thinking out there? Was she glad to be home? Or was she wishing she'd stayed in Pullman, where she was going to college? Maybe wishing she'd kept her job there over the summer so she wouldn't have to come back. So she could still see her boyfriend.

The hint of a smile on my lips melted into a scowl. Grace was dating some shithead at school. Actually, I had no idea if he was a shithead. She'd never brought him home, so I hadn't met him.

My eyes darted to the passenger seat of her car, an awful thought hitting me like a truck. Had she brought him with her?

My grip on the window trim tightened. The thought of spending the summer watching Grace with her college boyfriend made me want to put my fist through the glass.

Not that I had any right to be angry that she was dating someone.

Grace Miles was the literal girl next door. Sweet, pretty, and smart, with a stubborn streak that was as unshakable as the mountains we lived in. We'd grown up together. It hadn't been that long ago that the land surrounding our two houses had been our entire world. We'd been friends for most of our lives, but we'd never dated. And we certainly weren't dating now.

I released my grip on the window frame. Her passenger seat was empty. No boyfriend, shithead or otherwise.

Truthfully, I didn't want the guy to be a shithead. I wanted him to be great, because more than anything, I wanted Grace to be happy. She should have been dating a guy who was awesome —who treated her like a treasure. That was what she deserved.

"Stop licking the glass."

I whipped around and shot a glare at Logan. The floors up here creaked, so either my brother had been trying to sneak up on me, or I'd been too distracted to hear him. Probably the latter.

"How about I kick your ass?"

He grinned at me, the cocky little shit. Not that he was little anymore. He was eighteen, and we'd been the same height for a couple of years. My brothers and I—there were five of us—had inherited our father's stature. None of us were under six-two, even Gavin, who was only sixteen.

But I was the oldest, so I still had big brother power.

"I'll take a raincheck on that. I'm going out tonight. Don't want to mess this up." Logan gestured to his face. "Although a black eye is a great way to meet girls. Maybe I should take you up on it."

"You're an idiot."

He grinned again. "Maybe, but at least I'm not a stalker."

I stepped away from the window. "I'm not stalking her."

"Sure you're not."

Maybe I *would* give him a black eye. "Shut your face, asshole."

"Boys! Language." Gram's voice carried upstairs.

Logan and I furrowed our brows. We could start up our grandad's old truck, which had an engine so loud it rattled the windows, and she'd barely notice. But let us utter a single curse word above a whisper in Gram's house and she'd scold us like we were still kids.

"Sorry, Gram," I called down.

Logan wandered over to the window and glanced out. "Cool that she's home, though."

"Yeah."

Even without my face practically touching the glass, I could see her. She'd popped the trunk and pulled out a big suitcase. Her little brother, Elijah, burst out of the house and barreled into her, throwing his arms around her. She leaned down and kissed the top of his head.

"Quit being weird, dude." Logan said. "It's Grace."

"I know it's Grace, and I'm not being weird."

His forehead creased and he raised an eyebrow. "I can see that. Just like you're not stalking her."

Before he could react, I hooked an arm around his neck. I yanked him down, going for a headlock, but he twisted out of my grip and wrapped his arms around my waist. Driving with his legs, he pushed until my back crashed against the wall.

I got my feet under me and changed my grip on him. Lowering my center of gravity, I pivoted and flipped him over my shoulder. He landed hard on the bed, and his foot sent something on the bedside table crashing to the floor. I spun, getting chest to chest to maintain control. I'd wrestled in high school and now I took jiujitsu at an MMA gym in town, so my grappling skills were still sharp.

They had to be, in this family.

He grunted as I held him pinned down beneath my weight.

"Can you not break my stuff?"

A mirror image of Logan's face glared at us from the doorway. His twin, Levi, stood with his arms crossed. They looked a lot like me, but their features were more angular than mine, their cheekbones sharper. Even though they had identical DNA, I'd never had a problem telling them apart. Levi was so serious, whereas Logan always looked like he was up to something.

"Sorry." I stood and helped Logan up. This was the bedroom they shared, and I'd just body-slammed Logan onto Levi's bed.

Levi grunted and moved past me to pick up the lamp we'd knocked over. At least it didn't look like it was broken.

"Grace is home," Logan said.

"Yeah." Levi replied without looking at his brother.

"She needs a proper welcome. We should go give her a five-moon salute." Logan smirked and mimicked pulling his pants down to show his ass.

"Why would we do that?"

"Because it would be funny."

I shoved Logan. "Leave her alone."

"You two are boring as fuck," he said under his breath, then paused, as if waiting to see if Gram had heard him. The scolding didn't come, and he grinned. "Gavin'll do it with me."

I was about to tackle Logan again—or maybe Levi, just because—when the smell of strawberries wafted upstairs from the kitchen.

We all froze, sniffing the air, our eyes widening.

"Is Gram baking?" I asked.

Logan nodded. "Smells like—"

"Strawberry rhubarb," Levi finished.

I moved toward the door, but Logan knocked into me with his shoulder. Levi pushed past us both and we all scrambled to get to the kitchen first.

Our feet thundered on the old wooden staircase. We

shoved each other all the way down, as if we were a pack of
rowdy kids, not three guys who were technically adults. The
tantalizing scent grew. We burst into the kitchen just as
Gram pulled a pie out of the oven and set it on a wire rack
next to another. Despite the noise we'd just made rushing
down here, she only spared us a quick glance over her
shoulder.

Silver was replacing the black in Gram's long hair. She
wore it in a thick braid down her back, and had for as long
as I could remember. Although she'd recently turned
seventy, her dark skin was only just starting to show her age
and her posture was still straight. Kind of surprising, considering she'd had to unexpectedly raise five unruly boys, years
after having raised her own children.

She claimed it was the mountain air, copious amounts of
bacon, and her Native American ancestry that kept her
young. I tended to think she was simply too stubborn to let
age have its way with her.

For over two decades, my grandmother had been known
as Gram to everyone who knew her—related or not. But
before she'd married my grandad, Frank Bailey, she'd been
Emma Luscier, descendant of both the Chelan and
Wenatchi tribes. Her ancestors had lived in the Cascade
mountain range for countless generations.

Gavin already sat at the kitchen table, a wide rectangle
our grandad had built out of thick planks. The chairs placed
around it were sturdy, but worn from years of use. Grooves
in the wood floor marked the passage of two generations of
kids who'd grown up in this house.

Our youngest brother looked like a clone of the rest of
us. Dark hair, brown eyes, olive skin, and a semi-permanent
shit-eating grin. He was going through a phase of keeping
his hair so long it hung in his eyes, and he hadn't quite lost

his round cheeks yet. When I really wanted to piss him off, I called him babyface.

"The pie needs to cool," Gram said. "And there's no need to fight over it. I made plenty. Still have two more to bake."

The three of us hadn't tried to climb over each other to get downstairs because we thought we'd run out of pie. With five boys in the house, Gram always made enough food to feed an army. For us, it was just habit. We were brothers; wrestling was our love language.

Logan walked up behind her, put his hands on her shoulders, and kissed her cheek. "It just smells so good we can't help it. Plus, I'm starving."

"You just ate lunch."

"I ran five miles this morning." He leaned against the counter and grabbed an apple out of a bowl.

"Do you want a medal?" Levi asked.

Grinning, Logan tossed the apple at him. Levi caught it and threw it back.

"Go find Evan," Gram said.

Logan took a bite of the apple. "Which one of us?"

"All of you."

"Where is he?" Levi asked.

Gavin jerked his thumb toward the back door. "Woods. I saw him leave earlier."

Evan kept to himself a lot, often wandering in the woods out behind our house. He had come home from his second year of college a few days ago, but even though we shared a room when he was here, I hadn't seen much of him.

"Go on then," Gram said, shooing us with the oven mitt. "No pie until you bring your brother back, or you animals will eat it all before he has a chance at any."

A chorus of groans went around the kitchen, coupled with the scrape of Gavin's chair against the floor.

While my brothers headed for the door, I hung back. If Gram really wanted to be rid of all four of us, she'd shoo me out too. But I didn't want to wander the woods searching for Evan, so I hesitated next to the table, waiting to see if she'd insist I go.

She didn't.

The back door banged shut. I pulled out a chair and sat while she put two more pies in the oven.

"You finish up your finals?" she asked.

"Yep. All done until September."

"How'd you do?"

"Pretty sure I aced everything."

She closed the oven and put her oven mitts on the counter. "Of course you did."

Unlike Grace and my brother Evan, I'd stayed in town after high school and enrolled in Tilikum College. It was a good school, and had one of the best fire sciences programs in the state. Logan and Levi were starting there in the fall. All three of us planned on going into fire safety. I'd been a volunteer firefighter since I'd graduated high school, and my plan was to make a career of it. Eventually become a fire inspector. Maybe even fire chief someday.

But even if the college here hadn't been a good school, I still would have stayed. I couldn't leave Gram or my brothers. Our parents had died in an electrical fire when we were young—fortunately for us kids, we hadn't been in the house—and Gram and Grandad had taken us in.

We hadn't exactly made things easy on them. Whether it was just the nature of a family of five boys, or because we were all a little messed up from losing our parents—probably both—we'd been rowdy. Troublemakers, even.

Maturity was calming us down, at least a little. And I was doing my best to get—and keep—my shit together. As the oldest, it was my responsibility to be the man of the family, especially since Grandad had passed away a few years ago. I hadn't always done a great job at it, but I was trying.

However, I was seriously considering moving out—getting an apartment in town. I was twenty-one, three years out of high school, and itching to have my own place.

Still, I was worried about leaving, even if I'd only be a mile or two away.

Gram cut a piping hot piece of pie and brought it to the table. Slid it in front of me and handed me a fork with a wink.

"What troubles you, Bear?"

"Nothing."

"Hmm." She got her tea from the counter and sat across from me. "Grace is home for the summer."

"Yeah, I know."

"You could go next door and see her."

I took a bite of pie without meeting her eyes. "I'm sure she's busy. I'll see her at some point."

Gram didn't reply, just kept watching me eat.

"What?"

"Nothing." She took a sip of her tea.

"Gram, stop. You do this every time she comes home for a break. We're friends, but that's all."

"Friends can be excited to see each other when it's been a while."

I shrugged.

When she spoke again, her voice was soft. "It's okay to miss her, Bear."

She didn't mean miss her because I hadn't seen her since Christmas, and I knew it. She meant miss the way we used to be. We hadn't just been close, we'd been inseparable. As kids, Grace and I had been best friends. Basically glued to each other.

Not anymore.

We sat in silence for a while. Gram sipped her tea and I devoured the slice of pie. It was the perfect blend of tart and sweet, with a flaky crust that melted in my mouth.

I ate my last few bites, still thinking about Grace. The last time I'd seen her, the distance between us had felt like a canyon. It had sucked, but after she'd gone back to school, I'd mostly put her out of my mind. I was busy all the time, so that had made it easier. But now she was home, and I once again had to face the truth.

I had a thing for Grace. I had for a long time. And I'd never told her. Never told anyone.

I had my reasons, and it didn't matter now anyway. She was dating someone else. In a few short months, she'd go back to school. And maybe next summer would be the year she didn't come back home.

Thinking about a world without Grace—my world without her—was putting me in a shitty mood. Maybe I needed more pie.

"This was amazing." I gestured to my empty plate, then stood and took it to the counter where the pies were cooling.

"Don't even think about it, Bear." Gram wagged her finger at me. "You want more, you go pick me more strawberries."

"There's two more in the oven."

"I expect we'll have company soon." She paused to sip her tea. "In fact, go next door and ask Naomi and the kids to come on over before that wild pack of wolves you call brothers gets back."

I shot Gram a look. I should have known she'd have an ulterior motive for giving me the first slice of pie.

"Go on, now," she said, shooing me with her hand. "Don't make me tell you twice."

With a soft chuckle, I put my plate in the sink and lifted my hands in a gesture of surrender. "Okay, okay, I'm going."

I gave Gram a kiss on the head, then left to go tell Naomi and Elijah—and Grace—that we had pie.

3

GRACE

I always had mixed feelings when I came home from college.

On the one hand, it was good to see my family. My mom and I were close, and I missed her when I was away at school. My little brother, Elijah, was growing up so fast he was taller every time I saw him. And I really did like my hometown. I wasn't one of those people who'd left because I hated where I'd grown up. Tilikum was a quirky place, but it was home.

On the other hand, going away to college was a step forward, and coming home felt like taking two steps back. Like this house, and this town, resisted my efforts at growing up. I was trying to figure out who I was and what I wanted for my life. It was hard to do that here.

I pulled a stack of shirts out of my suitcase and set them in the open dresser drawer. Living in my childhood bedroom exacerbated the sense that I was being pulled backward in time. Not much about it had changed. Same twin bed shoved against a wall. Same pink comforter I'd had for years. Whitewashed dresser and nightstand with pink drawer pulls. A beat-up desk we'd found at a garage sale when I was twelve. I'd taken all my old posters down last year. They'd mostly been boy bands and a movie series I'd been obsessed with for a while. Now the walls were almost bare.

My eyes darted to the bulletin board in front of my desk. It was still covered with a collage of photos. Seventeen-year-old me holding a newborn Elijah. Another one of my little brother, taken last summer in Gram's kitchen. A few pictures of me with my high school girlfriends, including us in prom dresses. We'd gone as a group instead of taking dates.

But mostly, they were of me and Asher.

The two of us at the graduation party the Baileys had thrown for me in Gram's backyard. Sitting in the back of his grandad's old truck when we were in middle school. Us at ten and eleven, with dirty faces and skinned knees, hanging from the branches of the big tree out by the creek.

My favorite was one my mom had taken on my eighth birthday. Something had upset Asher—I couldn't remember now what it had been—and he'd gone outside by himself. I'd brought him a balloon to make him feel better. Mom had captured the moment I had handed it to him—the two of us standing apart, our arms outstretched, the balloon floating between us.

Leaving my suitcase half-unpacked, I wandered over to the window. My bedroom was the smallest in our little house, but I'd always insisted on keeping it. I'd wanted it for the view. This room faced Gram's house—and Asher's bedroom window.

As kids, we'd waved to each other from these windows. Signaled each other with flashlights after dark. Taped up

Happy Birthday and Merry Christmas signs for each other to see.

At some point, we'd stopped. But every time I came home, I still found myself gazing at his square of glass. Missing those times.

Missing him.

The last time I'd seen Asher had been at Christmas. It had been good to see him, but it had also been a painful reminder of how things had changed. How we'd grown apart.

It made me think of a story Gram had once told me, about a seed buried in the dirt. She'd said something inside the seed knew when the temperature was just right, and the sprout would break through the casing. Then it had to struggle through the soil for a while, pushing past pebbles and roots, before finally breaking the surface to find sunlight.

I hadn't understood what she'd meant at the time, but I thought I might now. Growing up was hard, and sometimes we had to struggle through the dirt to find our way. If Asher and I were both seedlings, we were finding separate paths to the surface of the soil. Ultimately, we'd both reach sunlight, just in different places.

"Hey, Grace?" My mom poked her head into my room. Her dark blond hair was in its usual ponytail, like she didn't have the time or energy to do anything else with it. She wore a light gray t-shirt and a pair of jeans she'd probably had since I was little. But even with her busy-single-mom wardrobe, she was beautiful. "I picked up some pizza for dinner. Want to come down?"

"Sure, I'll be there in a few minutes."

She smiled. "It's good to have you home."

"Thanks, Mom."

As ready as I'd been to find my own path to the sunlight, I hadn't taken the decision to go away to college lightly. There was a perfectly good school right here in Tilikum, and I could have saved money living at home. As the child of a single mother and a mostly-absent father, I'd been very conscious of the financial ramifications of college.

But I'd been dying for something new. A new place, new people, new experiences. And my mom had encouraged me to go away to college. Enthusiastically, in fact. I got the sense that she didn't want me to wind up stuck here, like her.

I glanced at Asher's window again. I'd never admitted it out loud, but he'd been the deciding factor. My senior year he'd been a freshman in college, and he'd started dating a girl he'd met at school. It had made me realize that staying here would mean watching Asher build a life with someone else. Even if it wasn't her—and ultimately, they hadn't stayed together—it would be someone. I wanted that for him. I wanted him to be happy. But living with it every day would be torture.

I'd spent high school working my ass off to get good grades. Participated in extracurricular activities to make my applications stronger. And applied for every scholarship under the sun.

And I'd done it. I'd gotten into WSU, a school four hours from home, with enough scholarships to make it work. Now I had two years of college under my belt. Two years of living somewhere else—in a place where no one knew my history. Where they didn't know my father had gotten my mom pregnant when she was nineteen, then dangled the possibility of marriage for years without ever committing. Where they didn't know I was the good girl. The overachiever who'd spent more time in high school building a resumé than hanging out with friends.

I'd started fresh. Made new friends. Done things no one who knew me here would believe. I'd gotten a fake ID and gone out to bars. Dyed my hair pink for a while. Gone to a frat party dressed as a mermaid. I'd taken a spontaneous road trip with a few friends to New York City over spring break. We'd taken turns at the wheel and gone over twenty-six hundred miles in forty-two hours. Spent a few days in the city, then drove all the way back across the country.

I'd even dated a couple of guys. Dating hadn't been on my radar in high school, so it had been a new experience for me. And it had been fun. Neither relationship had lasted very long, but I wasn't interested in getting serious with someone. And I was still friends with my most recent ex, so it had worked out fine.

Even with the fun I'd had—and I'd admittedly gone a little crazy, especially at first—I'd kept my grades up. I wasn't going to risk my scholarships. I had at least two more years until I finished my degree, and then... I didn't really know. The future still seemed like a hazy spot on the horizon—something I could just make out if I squinted. I wasn't sure what it was going to look like, only that I was determined to find my own road.

I put a few more things away—mostly clothes, plus books and other random stuff. I left some of it in the plastic tote I'd stuffed in the backseat of my car—just shoved it in a corner for now. There wasn't much point in unpacking everything when I'd just have to pack it all again in a few months.

Elijah ran up the stairs, making as much noise as a whole *pack* of almost-four-year-olds, not just one. He burst into my room, his dark hair hanging in his eyes.

"Are you coming?"

"Yeah, buddy, I'll be right there."

"Mom says it's time to eat."

"Okay, okay, I'm coming."

I followed Elijah down the stairs and through the cluttered living room. Toys spilled out of a toybox, littering the floor in front of the couch and armchairs. The furniture was newer than what we'd had when I was younger. My father had swooped back into my mom's life a couple of years before Elijah had come along, trying to win her back. He'd fixed things around the house and bought us new furniture. And for a little while, he'd had both of us fooled.

Then he'd taken us on a cruise, and nine months later, I had a baby brother. But Dad hadn't stuck around—because of course he hadn't. Mom had broken up with him for good —or what I hoped was for good—when Elijah was still a baby, and he'd gone back to being an absentee father who just paid child support.

I kind of hated the furniture. It was a constant reminder that I'd never been enough to make my dad stay.

The kitchen table, however, had been a gift from Gram and Grandad Bailey when I was little. It was round with dark brown stain and four matching chairs. I trailed my hands along the back of one of the chairs as I walked by.

Mom was in the kitchen, busy pouring Elijah a glass of milk. The pizza box sat on the counter.

"I hope you still like pepperoni," Mom said.

I saw the name on the box—Home Slice Pizza—and my brow furrowed. "Pepperoni is fine, but you can't get pizza there. The Havens own that place."

She pulled three plates out of the cupboard and set them on the counter. "Oh, lord. Grace, I don't have time to worry about who owns what pizza place or what side they're on. That stupid feud is ridiculous anyway."

I eyed the pizza box with suspicion, like there might be a rattlesnake inside.

She wasn't wrong. The Tilikum town feud *was* ridiculous. But the fact that it was ridiculous had nothing to do with loyalty.

Tilikum was a town divided. The college and surrounding area were generally regarded as neutral territory, but the rest of the town was split. It had been that way for generations, and it influenced everything. Where you shopped and ate. Who your friends were. Where you worked. Even where you lived. It all depended on which side you chose, or had been chosen for you by the family of your birth.

Baileys or Havens.

The true origins of the feud were lost to the murky depths of history and town lore. Some said it had started with a murder. Others said it had started with an affair. There were stories about treasure buried somewhere in the mountains. About a young couple hopping a train and disappearing forever, leaving angry families behind. The theories were as divisive as the feud itself. Everyone in town had a favorite, and debates could get heated.

These days, the feud wasn't nearly as dramatic as runaway lovers or torrid affairs. And there were certainly no murders. Even so, lines had been drawn.

As for me, I'd always been on Team Bailey, and my loyalty was fierce.

"I already bought it," she said. "What difference does it make?"

Elijah crossed his arms. "I don't want it."

Mom put a slice on a plate and shot me a look.

I grabbed the plate and took it to the table. "Come on,

Eli. Mom didn't mean to get the wrong pizza, and it wouldn't be right to waste it."

His little brow creased. "Will they be mad?"

"Who?"

"The Baileys."

I reached out and ruffled his hair. "No, buddy. They won't be mad. They'd eat the pizza, too."

That seemed to convince him. He slid into the chair and started shoveling pizza into his mouth.

I got a slice for myself and Mom joined us at the table with hers.

"Speaking of Baileys, I'm surprised they're not crawling all over this place, what with you being home," Mom said.

I shrugged. "We're not kids anymore. It's not like they're going to come running out the front door when I pull up."

"I'm gonna be a firefighter when I grow up," Elijah said through a mouthful of pizza.

"Are you?" I asked.

He nodded, making his hair flop on his forehead. "Just like Asher. And Logan and Levi."

Mom sighed. "He'd follow those boys around like a puppy if I let him. Wants to do everything they do."

"What's your third-favorite dinosaur?" he asked.

"I..." My brow furrowed. "I have no idea. What's your third-favorite dinosaur?"

"T-rex." He took another bite.

Mom shrugged. Apparently third-favorite dinosaur was a normal question coming from him. "How's Daniel? Does he miss you already?"

I wiped my mouth on a napkin. "Oh, no. We broke up a little while ago."

"You did? I'm sorry. He seemed nice from everything you said about him."

"It's okay. He was nice, but it wasn't serious. And we're still friends."

"You sure you're okay?"

"Yes, Mom, I'm fine."

"Who's Daniel?" Elijah asked.

"He was Grace's boyfriend," Mom said.

Elijah set his pizza crust on his plate, his expression serious. "Is a boyfriend like getting married?"

"Not necessarily," Mom said. "Sometimes a boy and a girl like each other a lot and spend time together. And they might get married someday, but they might not."

"Oh. Okay, because Grace is gonna marry Asher."

I met my mom's eyes right as a flush hit my cheeks. "What?"

Mom's lips curled in an amused smile. "Is she? What makes you think that?"

"She just is. Can I have more pizza?"

"I'll get it." I took his plate and got up, glad for an excuse to leave the table.

Why had that flustered me so much? I should have been able to laugh off his comment. He wasn't even four; what did he know?

But there had been a time when I'd thought I *would* marry Asher Bailey.

I'd already accepted that Asher didn't see me that way. We'd grown up together. How could a guy be attracted to a girl when he'd caught frogs in a creek and rolled down grassy hills with her? When they'd pummeled each other with snowballs and built forts in the woods together? I was probably like a sister to him.

His brothers certainly treated me like a sister, and that had always felt natural. They basically *were* my brothers.

But Asher... he'd always been different. I'd never seen

him as a brother, not even when we were little kids. Best friend? Yes. Brother? No.

By the time I'd reached my teens, I'd started noticing things about him. The muscles in his arms and his thick, athletic thighs. His deep brown eyes, sharp cheekbones, and chiseled jaw. His charming smile. Asher was gorgeous and it had been impossible not to develop a crush on my best friend.

But he hadn't felt the same. In fact, the older we'd gotten, the more we'd grown apart. Looking back, I figured it was just how these things happened. He'd wanted to date girls, not climb trees and splash in mud puddles with one. And since he hadn't wanted to date *me*, here we were.

I glanced back at Elijah. He was too young to remember the days when Asher and I had been inseparable. So what had given him the idea that we were going to get married?

It was probably because the circle of people Eli knew mostly included me, Mom, and the Baileys. He didn't realize there was a whole world of people out there, and that growing up next door to someone didn't mean you'd marry each other someday.

Someone knocked on the front door and Elijah popped out of his chair. "I wanna get it!"

I put Eli's second piece of pizza at his now-empty place at the table. He threw open the door and a little thrill of excitement I didn't want to feel made my stomach flutter.

It was Asher.

4

ASHER

"Asher!" Elijah said, throwing the door open. "We have pizza and Grace is home."

"Hey, buddy." I ruffled his hair, but my attention was only partially on him.

Grace stood next to their kitchen table with her hand on a chair. Her hair was up in that cute ponytail she always wore, and her feet were bare. She had bright blue eyes and an upturned nose, and her full lips parted when she smiled at me.

Damn, those eyes. And that smile. She lit up the whole room.

I opened my mouth to say hi—I needed to stop staring at her before this got weird—but Elijah hooked his hands around my forearm and lifted his legs, hanging from my arm like it was a tree branch.

"Whoa." I flexed to keep him steady and lifted him off the ground. "There's a monkey on my arm."

"Eli, don't do that," Grace said.

I carried him inside, his feet dangling. "It's too bad there's only this monkey here and no little boys."

Elijah laughed. "Why?"

"Because Gram made pie, and monkeys don't get pie."

His feet hit the floor and he let go. "I'm a boy. Can I have some?"

"I don't know. You'll have to go ask Gram."

Without another word, he dashed out the open door.

"Sorry if I ruined his dinner. Gram asked me to invite you over for pie before my brothers eat it all." I gestured over my shoulder, jerking my thumb in the direction of our house.

"It's fine; at least he ate one slice." Naomi smiled and stood, wiping her hands on a napkin. "I better bring his shoes, since he ran off in socks."

My gaze went to Grace again while Naomi grabbed Eli's shoes and left. She'd moved toward me, or I'd moved toward her, or maybe both. For some reason it was kind of hard to tell what was happening, except that we were now only about a foot apart.

"Hey. Good to see you."

The corners of her mouth lifted and something in her eyes tugged at me. "You too."

The air felt thick, like there was an invisible barrier between us. She was only a step away, but it might as well have been a mile. I didn't like it.

I opened my arms and stepped in for a hug. She popped up on her tiptoes and wound her arms around my neck.

Uh-oh.

I'd hugged Grace a million times, but this felt different. We were different. She wasn't the girl in pigtails who'd probably punch me in the arm after I let go. She was a woman. A woman who felt dangerously good with her body pressed against mine.

Closing my eyes, I inhaled her scent and flexed to wrap

my arms tighter around her. I needed to let go. I was going to make things awkward if I kept hugging her like this. Because this wasn't the kind of hug you gave a friend you hadn't seen in a while. There was nothing friendly about it —not on my end at least.

God, I'd missed her.

I reveled in a few more seconds of contact, then dropped my arms. Hers slid from my shoulders and she took a step back.

"So..." She glanced away and tightened her ponytail. "Gram made pie?"

I was a little lightheaded after that hug, but I didn't want her to notice. "Yeah, everybody wants to see you, so I guess we should go next door."

She moved past me to slip her feet into her flip-flops. "How was spring semester?"

"Good. I had a couple of tough classes, so I'm glad it's over."

"Yeah, me too. How's Gram?"

I followed her out the door. "She's fine. Same as always."

"Good. I missed her."

"Yeah, she missed you too."

She glanced at me while we walked side by side. For a second, I hoped she'd say she'd missed me, too. That would certainly give me a reason to say it back. But she just looked away and kept walking across the grass.

As soon as we stepped onto the porch, I could tell my brothers had beat us back. Noise poured out the open front door. The chorus of male voices was cut by a squeal from Elijah and Naomi's laughter. Grace and I paused, sharing a look before we walked into the chaos.

Gram's kitchen always looked right when it was full of people. Like it was meant for that, in a way other kitchens weren't. Elijah sat at the head of the table, happily eating a giant slice of pie. Logan sat next to him, grinning at whatever Eli had just said. Gavin leaned against the counter, his plate held up close to his face while he ate. Even Levi's perpetual brow furrow had smoothed, his usual surliness softened by Gram's famous strawberry rhubarb pie.

My brothers had obviously found Evan. He sat at the table, but even sitting, he looked huge. At six-foot-four and with shoulders as wide as a barn, he seemed to tower over everyone. He was only a year younger than me, but he'd shot past me in height a few years ago. We Baileys were big guys, but Evan took big to a whole new level.

"Grace!"

I wasn't sure who shouted her name first. But a second later, she was being hugged by all my brothers. Elijah jumped down from his seat to wrap his arms around anyone's legs he could find. The little guy always wanted to be in on the action.

And all this, right here, was what had kept me from ever making a move with Grace. She was a part of this family. So were her mom and her little brother. Our lives, and the lives of everyone we both loved, were tightly intertwined.

My sense of responsibility to my family, and hers, had always held me back. Because what if something went wrong? What if Grace and I dated and it didn't work out—then what? I'd grown up in a town divided by a feud started by people long dead for reasons no one could remember—a community still haunted by the rift between two families. Even back in high school, I'd known I couldn't risk tearing our families apart.

That had always seemed like a good reason to stay friends and leave it at that. But looking at her now, while she smiled and traded hugs with my brothers, I wondered if I'd been wrong. If I'd made a mistake and missed my chance with her.

Because what if we dated, and it *did* work out?

I'd been with a few girls since high school, but never anything serious. Deep down, I knew the reason wasn't them. It was me. I never let things get serious—always broke it off before the relationship could really go anywhere.

The problem was, Grace had lodged herself into my heart a long time ago, and she hadn't left room for anyone else to get in.

That was a fucked-up realization to have while standing in Gram's kitchen, surrounded by all the reasons I'd never made a move.

I watched her smile and laugh. Hug everyone and tell them that school was great. She loved it and she couldn't wait to go back in the fall.

Looking down, I realized Gram was trying to hand me a plate with a slice of pie. Damn it, I'd been staring at Grace. I took it, absently grabbing the fork.

"You look like you could use another slice," Gram said.

I nodded, feeling oddly tongue-tied. Something was wrong with me. I didn't feel like myself. Ever since I'd hugged Grace next door, it was like I'd come unhinged. Dangerous impulses kept trying to overtake me. I wanted to wrap my arms around her again. Grab her hand, haul her out to the back porch, and kiss the hell out of her. Or maybe kiss her right here, in front of everyone.

"I'm sorry I couldn't make it back for graduation," Grace was saying to Logan and Levi. "It just didn't work with finals and everything."

"That's okay, graduation was boring," Logan said. "We waited for you to get home to throw a grad party, anyway."

She smiled. "You did? Thanks."

"Yeah, we figured we'd have it later this summer. Keep the celebration going." Logan smirked at her. "So when are you going to dump that college boy and go out with me?"

Levi rolled his eyes and threw a wadded-up napkin at him. Logan batted it to the floor.

Grace laughed. "We're not together anymore. But sorry, Logan, I'm not into younger guys."

"What? I'm only two years younger than you, and very mature for my age."

Levi and Evan both snorted. Even Gram stifled a laugh.

Logan put a hand on his chest. "I'm hurt. But that's okay, I wouldn't date you anyway."

Grace crossed her arms. "Why not?"

"You're cute and everything, but I'm not into older women."

"That's because you couldn't handle this woman," she said.

Levi whistled and everyone laughed—everyone except me. I was back to staring at Grace, my pie untouched, the fork dangling from my fingers.

She'd just said *We're not together anymore.*

Her eyes darted to me and she winked. She'd probably just scored another zinger on Logan, which was always hilarious because Logan could dish it out better than he could take it. My mouth hooked in a smile, and I winked back at her. But it wasn't because I was sharing in the humor of her snarking at my brother.

It was because I'd just realized two things.

One, Grace was single. Not only was she single, but the way she'd said *We're not together anymore* told me everything I needed to know about her breakup with the shithead. She wasn't upset. I knew her. If she'd been brokenhearted, I'd have been able to tell. Which meant either it hadn't been very serious, or she'd been the one to break up with him. Maybe both.

Two, I didn't just have a thing for Grace. I was in love with her.

Crazy fucking in love with her.

It was a fact I'd been denying for a long time. Telling myself the distance between us was because we'd grown apart. That wasn't true. I'd *put* that distance between us. Pulled away from her because I thought my feelings for her were too dangerous.

I'd been wrong. Loving her wasn't dangerous. Letting her go would be.

Feeling suddenly better than I had in a long time, I took a bite of pie, my eyes still on Grace. I wasn't going to kiss her right now. Not here or on the back porch. Not yet.

I could, and a big part of me wanted to. But I didn't want to leave any room for her to doubt me, or to doubt us.

She'd be going back to school in the fall. The longer she spent away from home, the more likely it was that she wouldn't just date someone else, she'd meet *the* someone else. The guy who'd take her away from me forever.

Which meant I had to do this right. I couldn't just kiss her and hope she felt something for me too. I couldn't leave it up to chance. I had to work for it. Show her how great we'd be together.

I had to chase her.

Grace didn't know it yet, but she was mine. Long before the end of summer, she'd know. And she'd know I was hers, too.

5

GRACE

*S*omething tapped against my bedroom window and I spun around to look. Nothing. I was on the second story, and the tree branch that had once grown close enough to scrape against it in the wind had long since been trimmed. I hoped a bird hadn't flown into the glass, although that would have made a thud, not a tap.

I heard it again and my eyes caught movement this time. I went over to the window and looked down. Asher stood below, looking up, his arm cocked like he was about to throw something.

What was he doing down there?

I opened the window and leaned out. "Are you throwing rocks at my window?"

Grinning, he lowered his arm. "Yeah."

"Why?"

"Do you have to work today?"

I was returning to my summer job at the local coffee shop, the Steaming Mug. "Nope. I don't start until tomorrow."

"Wanna sneak out with me?"

Sneak out? What was he talking about? "Asher, my mom isn't even home. And I'm twenty. I don't need to sneak out of my house."

He smiled again, making his dimples pucker. "I thought it would be fun. Come on."

"You want me to climb out my window?"

He nodded. "Yeah."

This wouldn't have been the first time I'd climbed out my window to meet Asher. But it had been years. I'd been smaller, and more nimble, the last time I'd done this.

But he was right—it would be fun.

"If I fall, you better catch me."

He smiled again and held his arms out. "You know I will, Gracie Bear."

Hearing him use my nickname sent a flutter through my stomach. He hadn't called me that in a long time.

"Okay, hold on."

I put on a pair of shoes and climbed out onto the ledge below my window. Plastering myself against the siding, I inched my way across, until I was close to the porch roof.

The first time I'd done this, it had been my idea. Asher had crept along below, whispering words of encouragement in the dark. The sun was still up this time, but my heart beat against my ribs. I stretched my toe toward the porch roof, then eased my body weight toward that foot. When I felt secure, I pushed off and landed on the sloped surface with bent knees.

"Nice one," Asher said below me.

I crept down the edge of the roof and turned around, getting on my stomach. Sliding down, I let my legs dangle over the side.

"I've got you."

The ground sloped upward on this side of the house just

enough that he could reach me as I dropped from the porch roof. I felt his hands on my calves, then my thighs as I slid lower. His arms wrapped around the tops of my legs and the next thing I knew, I was sliding down the front of his body.

My feet hit the ground and he kept his arms around me. I froze, my body stiffening. For a second, the world seemed to pause. The breeze stilled and the birds quieted. Warmth spread through me, and it wasn't just the heat of Asher's body pressed so close to mine. With his arms wrapped around me, I could feel him, smell him. It was overwhelming.

Confusing.

Arousing.

He let go and the breath rushed from my lungs. I stepped away, keeping my back to him, and fixed my ponytail to give myself a second to recover.

What the heck had just happened?

I didn't want to let this sudden rush of feelings show, especially since Asher wanted to hang out, and we hadn't done that in a long time. Not just the two of us. I didn't want to ruin it.

So I took a deep breath to clear my head and turned around. "Where are we sneaking off to?"

"I have a few ideas." He grabbed my hand. "Let's go."

And now he was holding my hand.

He led me around the back of Gram's house, like we really were trying to sneak away without being seen. When we got near the front, he put his fingers to his lips, prompting me to be quiet. Stifling a laugh, I nodded. He was so funny.

We tiptoed to his car—he still drove the old black Cutlass he'd bought from one of his uncles. He let me in the passenger's side, then shut the door. With an exaggerated gait, he walked around to the other side and got in. Put his fingers to his lips again and winked.

I covered my mouth to keep from laughing. He was being so ridiculous. He made a show of looking around, then turned on the car.

As soon as the engine kicked over, he tore out of the driveway like we'd just robbed a bank. He looked in the rear-view mirror, as if expecting to be followed. I had no idea why that was so funny, but I couldn't stop laughing.

"I think we made a clean getaway," I said.

He glanced over his shoulder. "I think you're right. Nice work."

We only lived about a mile outside the main part of town. As kids, we'd walked everywhere. To the Sugar Shack, our pockets stuffed with change to buy gum and penny-candy. To the library or the community pool. Tilikum was still the sort of place where kids could roam free. It made me glad my mom had stayed and was raising my brother here. It was a good place for a kid to grow up.

Asher parked near City Hall, on a flat street just before the hill sloped down toward the river. We got out and stepped up onto the sidewalk. It could get hot on the eastern slopes of the Cascades during the summer, but today was comfortably warm. A few clouds hung in the blue sky and the air was still.

"So what did you have in mind?"

"I thought we could ruin our dinner with ice cream from the Zany Zebra, then go hang out at the Caboose. Shoot some pool."

"Ruin our dinner? You sound like Gram."

"It rubs off on you." He stuffed his hands in his pockets and shrugged. "I just figured it might be nice to get out of the house for a while."

He was right—getting out of the house was nice. My mom was at work and Elijah was with the babysitter. I didn't have much of a Tilikum social life anymore. Most of the people I'd been friends with in high school had left—seeds scattered in the wind, off to find their way to the surface in new places.

"I could go for some ice cream."

He smiled at me, those dimples puckering again. "Great."

I needed to stop thinking about how cute his dimples were.

We wandered down the sidewalk side by side, in comfortable silence. Asher kept his hands in his pockets, and I suppressed a tiny flicker of disappointment. But what did I want him to do, hold my hand? Asher and I weren't like that.

Besides, I was only here for the summer. Even if this strange electricity between us was real—which it wasn't—nothing could happen. I wasn't staying. A summer fling was all well and good, but Asher could never be a fling. We had too much history together. Deep down, I knew that there were only two ways my relationship with Asher could go. Either we stayed friends and lived our own lives, or we lived a life together.

I'd given up on the second possibility already. So I needed to keep my head out of the clouds and my feet planted firmly on the ground.

We came to a white building painted with black stripes. Zany Zebra had been a fixture in Tilikum since before my mom was born. It served cheap, greasy burgers, the best waffle fries ever, and a selection of house-made ice cream.

I got a cone with a scoop of mountain blackberry. Asher

chose double fudge chocolate. We took our ice cream with us and wandered deeper into town.

Gerald McMillan came out the open door to his barbershop, adorably named The Art of Manliness. An old-fashioned barber pole twirled on the side of the building. Mr. McMillan didn't have much of his auburn hair left, but he had a thick, well-groomed beard, and wore a crisp white apron.

Asher paused and held up a hand. "Hi, Mr. McMillan."

"Hey, Asher." His deep voice rumbled. "Hi, Grace. You must be home from school."

"Yep, I got back yesterday. How's business?"

"Oh, you know, I can't complain. Except for that bastard Bruce Haven." He leveled a glare at the building kitty-corner from his shop.

I glanced at Tilikum's other barbershop. As a feuding town, we had two of most things—one for people on the Bailey side and one for the Havens—and the businesses fought over the customers in between. Bruce Haven owned the Dame and Dapper Barbershop, and he and Mr. McMillan had a long history of trying to outdo—and annoy—each other.

Outside the Dame and Dapper stood a huge painted statue of a vintage pinup girl. She wore a red dress that showed a lot of cleavage, fishnet stockings and high heels, and looked like she was blowing soap suds off her hand.

"When did he put that up?" I asked.

Mr. McMillian crossed his arms over his barrel chest. "Few months ago. Damn statue."

"I can't believe the town council let him do that."

"Doubt he asked permission," he grumbled.

"What are you going to do to get him back?"

The corner of his mouth turned up. "Oh, don't you worry about that. I have a few more tricks up my sleeve."

I laughed. "Sounds good."

"You want me to have my brothers put a beard on her?" Asher asked.

"Not a bad idea."

"I might accidentally mention something."

Mr. McMillan winked. "I don't know anything about it."

Asher put his hands up. "Me neither. I'm just taking Grace out for ice cream."

"You two have a nice afternoon."

"Thanks, Mr. McMillian," I said.

We kept walking down the sidewalk, licking our cones to keep them from dripping. I nudged Asher with my elbow.

"Put a beard on her?"

"I have no idea what you're talking about."

I laughed. "I'm just surprised you guys haven't done it already."

"Yeah, well, we've all been busy, so..."

Asher and his brothers had always taken their pranks seriously, feud-related or otherwise.

By the time we got to the Caboose, we'd both finished our ice cream. Asher held the door for me, and we went inside.

The Caboose had originally been built to look like an old-fashioned railroad car. About ten years ago the owners, Hank and Jeannie Chesterton, had expanded it, giving them more square footage. The building no longer looked like an actual caboose, but they'd kept the bright red paint.

Inside, it was decorated with old railroad signs and model trains. It was half bar, half restaurant, with a partial wall separating the bar area. The restaurant side had a mix of tables and booths, with dark wood and red vinyl seats, plus an open section with two pool tables and some vintage arcade games.

It was mostly empty, just a small group sitting in one of the booths, and a couple of old-timers holding down stools over at the bar.

"Want to eat first, or play some pool?" Asher asked.

"I think the ice cream did ruin my dinner."

He grinned. "We can wait. I'll go get us a pitcher of Coke."

I watched him walk away and it was impossible not to notice the way his muscular back and arms filled out his t-shirt. And his ass. God.

Watching his ass in those jeans, I found myself wondering what it would be like to let him do dirty things to me. Dirty things I'd never done with anyone. Although I'd fooled around a bit with both of my exes, I hadn't slept with either of them. But my lack of sexual experience didn't mean I couldn't imagine.

Oh my god, what was I doing? This was Asher. My cheeks warmed and I tore my gaze away from him while I moved to one of the pool tables. Yes, he was attractive. He was thick and strong and capable. His understated confidence was stupidly sexy.

How the hell was he single?

Wait, *was* he single?

He'd been dating someone when I'd been home over the holidays. I'd overheard Logan asking him if he thought he was getting a blow job for Christmas. I'd walked away too quickly to hear his reply. I hadn't wanted to know.

It didn't seem like he was dating her now, but it was hard to tell. We hadn't exactly been confiding in each other about our relationships—or anything, really—over the last few years. I knew he dated girls, and I assumed he knew I'd dated those guys at school. But it wasn't something we'd talked about.

He came back with our drinks and set them on a table.

"Ready to lose?" he asked.

"You're awfully confident."

"I've seen you play."

I gave him a playful shove and he grinned at me.

Was I imagining the heat in his gaze as he handed me a pool cue? The quick sweep of his eyes and twitch of his lips as if he liked what he saw? I must have been, because Asher never looked at me like that.

He also never kept his arms around me like when he'd helped me off the roof. Or hugged me the way he had yesterday at my mom's house.

Now I was just letting my imagination run away with me.

We started our game and unfortunately for me, Asher wasn't wrong. I was pretty terrible at pool. In between attempting to sink a ball into one of the pockets and his good-natured teasing, I couldn't stop thinking about whether he had a girlfriend. Which was silly. I didn't need to be preoccupied with Asher's relationship status. It didn't have anything to do with me.

Plus, I wanted him to be happy. Even though we'd grown apart, I still cared about him.

Maybe that was a good enough reason to ask. We were friends. Friends talked about that sort of thing. What if she'd left for the summer and he missed her? Or they'd broken up recently and he was trying to hide the fact that he was sad about it? Although I doubted he'd be able to hide that from me. I knew him too well, and he didn't seem sad.

At this point, I was starting to drive myself crazy, so I just blurted out the question. "Are you still dating that girl you were with at Christmas?"

He stopped, his pool cue resting on the edge of the table, and looked at me with lifted eyebrows. "No. We broke up a while ago."

"Oh. That sucks. I'm sorry."

He watched me for a second, then turned his attention back to the game. Took his shot and missed. "It's okay, it wasn't a big deal. Sometimes things just don't work out."

"Yeah." I walked around the table, looking for a good shot. Not that I knew much about what I was looking for.

"What about you?" He leaned his hip against the table. "Did you and your boyfriend decide to take a break for the summer?"

"No, he and I are better as friends." I lined up my pool cue and took a shot. The ball actually went in. "And I'm not really looking for anything serious right now."

"Why not? Think you're too young?"

I considered his question as I lined up another shot. "No, it's not that. I'm just focused on other things. I need to finish college, and then..."

"And then?"

I hit the cue ball but the three bounced off the side, slowing to a stop in the middle of the table. "And then, I don't really know. I'm not sure what I want to do with my life yet."

"Really? No ideas?"

"I have ideas, I guess. But I'm open to the possibilities."

The corner of his mouth twitched upward. "Good."

Suddenly I wondered if we were talking about career choices, or something else.

"My mom would like it if I had a better idea of what I want to do with my life."

He laughed softly. "You're going to be successful at whatever you set your mind to. I know you, Gracie Bear. That's how you operate. You're too stubborn to fail."

The warmth of his approval spread through me. I hadn't realized how much I needed to hear that. "Thanks, Asher."

He smiled at me, and my gaze locked with his. With those deep, dark brown eyes. His lips twitched, puckering his dimples, and the fluttering in my stomach was back—with a vengeance.

The door opened, the sound breaking my trance. Cory Wilcox and Joel Decker walked in. Asher glanced over and his eyes narrowed. We'd gone to school with both of them; they'd graduated with Asher's class. As far as I knew, Cory worked construction and Joel had gone to work for his dad's auto body shop.

At the sight of them, I didn't just narrow my eyes. I downright glared.

They were friends with the Havens.

"Easy, tiger," Asher said. "That death glare of yours is liable to hurt someone."

"I don't have a death glare."

"No? I wouldn't want to be on the other end of it."

I wasn't so petty that I disliked half my town simply because of some old feud. There were plenty of people on the Haven side who were perfectly decent. Several of my teachers growing up had been Havens. There was an unspoken truce when it came to teachers, police officers, firefighters, and healthcare workers. We weren't backwards hicks who'd deny someone medical attention or a proper education just because they were on the other side.

And most of the time, the feud was as silly as it was old. It was played out with harmless pranks, competition for prizes at town festivals, and a whole lot of trash-talking.

But Cory and Joel? Guys like them made it into something worse. Used it as an excuse to be assholes and start trouble.

"Why do you think they're here?" I asked.

"Who knows. Maybe a dare." He chalked the end of his cue. "Just ignore them. They'll get bored and leave."

Hank stood behind the bar and crossed his arms. Cory and Joel both glanced in our direction, then walked over to the bar. Asher took his shot and the balls clacked.

"You're up, Gracie Bear."

I lined up my shot, trying to ignore the intruders. "Do you think Hank'll serve them?"

"He will if they show some manners. But I doubt they will, so probably not."

My cue hit and the balls thwacked together, but I didn't come close to sinking any of them.

"Are you trying to hustle me, or are you still this bad?" Asher asked.

"Shut up, Bailey."

He grinned. Although his posture was relaxed, I saw his eyes flick to Cory and Joel again, like he was casually keeping track of them. He put the five in the corner pocket, then missed his next shot.

"Your turn."

I leaned over the table to take my turn, but Cory and Joel headed our direction. I straightened, wrapping both my hands around the cue.

Asher didn't look concerned, but I was.

Scuffles didn't break out over the feud very often, but it could happen. If these guys were here to pick a fight, I knew Asher could handle it, even if it was two on one. He'd been a district champion wrestler, and now he competed in jiujitsu tournaments around the state. I wasn't worried he'd get hurt.

I was worried because Asher could *not* get in trouble with the law again. Not if he was going to get his juvenile records sealed. And he had to, or his dreams of being a fire-fighter would be smashed to pieces. Even an arrest with no charges could ruin everything for him.

When he was seventeen, Asher had gotten in a fight with Josiah Haven outside the Zany Zebra on a Friday night. I hadn't been there to see it, but a bunch of kids had recorded it on their phones. By the time someone had broken it up, Asher's nose had been bloodied. And he'd broken Josiah's arm.

He'd been arrested and charged with assault. A felony. Fortunately, he hadn't been charged as an adult. The judge had ordered him to complete a counseling program and community service hours instead of sending him to jail, so it hadn't interfered with graduating high school on time. But now he had to wait five years from the time of his arrest to have the records sealed. Until then, he was technically a felon with a criminal record.

I also happened to know that Asher had gotten in that fight to protect his brother, Evan.

My heart sank as Cory and Joel stopped next to our pool table.

"Sup, Bailey."

Asher's forearms flexed as he wrapped his hands around his cue. "You guys need something, or you just in here to prove you have the balls for it?"

"Just seeing what the deal is," Joel said. "Heard this place has good onion rings."

"It does."

"Too bad the owner's a dick."

Asher turned his attention back to the table, effectively dismissing them.

There was a pause, the only sound the music from the old-fashioned jukebox. Hank still stood behind the bar, watching. Cory and Joel seemed to realize they weren't going to get the reaction they were looking for—whatever that was— from Asher.

Cory nodded toward the door. "Let's get out of this shithole."

But Joel's gaze swung to me. "Hey, Grace."

"Why don't you guys go cause trouble somewhere else?" I said. "We're just trying to play."

"No one's causing trouble, beautiful."

Asher's jaw hitched and his voice was low. "Don't call her that."

Like a couple of sharks detecting the irresistible scent of blood in the water, they zeroed in on Asher.

"You gonna do something about it, Bailey?" Joel asked.

Asher didn't move. He kept his hands around the cue, the muscles in his shoulders and arms bunching with tension, and stared them down.

"No?" Joel's gaze slid to me. "If he's not giving it to you good enough, I will."

Cory grabbed his crotch. "Why don't you come take this for a ride, baby?"

"Gross, Cory," I said. "How would I even find it? I don't have a magnifying glass with me."

Joel chuckled, but it took Cory a second for my insult to sink in.

"You stupid bitch." Cory took a step toward me, but Asher smoothly inserted himself between me and the jackass.

"Don't." Asher's voice was dangerously low.

The air was so thick with tension, I could barely breathe. My heart beat hard and my pulse throbbed in my temples. I could feel Asher straining to keep himself in check.

The door flew open again and more voices spilled into the quiet restaurant. Logan strutted in, laughing—probably at his own joke. He was followed by Levi, who was rolling his eyes—probably at the same joke. They stopped, spotting us, and the smile melted from Logan's face.

"The fuck's going on over here?" Logan asked, striding over to us with undisguised confidence.

Levi was quieter, but the look he gave Cory and Joel was menacing. He stopped and crossed his arms.

"They were just leaving," Asher said.

Like the bullies they were, the two jackasses seemed to decide they didn't like these odds. Both lost their aggressive posture and moved back.

Joel smiled. "We were just messing with you."

Asher didn't reply. The anger coming off him was palpable.

"Let's get out of here," Cory said.

As if he had something to prove, Joel leered at me and winked.

Asher jerked forward, but I sprang around him and put a hand on his chest. Less than a second later, Levi was there.

"Easy," Levi said quietly.

Cory and Joel turned to go. Logan didn't move out of their way. Joel knocked his shoulder into Logan's as he walked by, but it was like he'd hit a brick wall. Logan didn't move. He just laughed.

They left, but Asher's eyes stayed locked on the door. His body was tense, his fists clenched. I knew what he was thinking. He wanted to follow them out.

Levi put a hand on his shoulder. "Let it go, man."

Asher's gaze moved to me. The intensity glittering in his eyes softened.

"They're just jerks," I said. "Come on. You were beating me at pool, remember?"

My hand was still on his chest and I felt him take a deep breath. He was so imposing. So solid and strong. His dark eyes held me captive and my stomach was suddenly a whirlpool. Why was he looking at me like that?

"So what's up?" Logan asked. "Are you guys going to finish your game?"

Gasping, I dropped my hand.

"Yeah." Asher's lips twitched in a grateful smile, and he lowered his voice. "Thanks."

"No problem."

With another deep breath, he went back to the pool table.

Feeling a little jittery—I didn't know whether it was from the feel of my hand on Asher's chest and the look in his eyes, or the almost-altercation—I went back to our game.

And I wondered if what had just passed between us had been real, or in my imagination.

6

ASHER

*I*t was quiet at the firehouse today. Some of the guys had gone out on a call—a fender bender on the highway just north of town. I wasn't on duty, and they hadn't needed any extra hands, so I'd stayed behind.

I'd been a volunteer firefighter since shortly after I'd graduated high school. I worked part time at the hardware store, but when I wasn't training at the gym, working, or in class, I was here. This place was basically a second home to me. If I wasn't on duty, I studied or did homework. It was good experience and it kept me out of trouble.

I sat at a table in the big kitchen upstairs, a few books spread out in front of me. In addition to my college classes, I had exams to pass for my certifications. I couldn't take the tests until next year—I had to wait for my juvenile record to be sealed first—but I figured I should stay up on the material.

"Asher." Chief Stanley set his coffee down and took the seat across from me. "I didn't realize anyone was in here."

Norman Stanley had been Tilikum's fire chief for over a decade. He'd grown up here in town, and started with the fire department as a volunteer when he was nineteen. He'd also been my dad's best friend.

I tapped the book in front of me. "Just reviewing a few things. Figured I should keep it fresh."

He took a sip of his coffee and nodded. "You'll do fine when the time comes."

Chief Stanley had been one of my biggest advocates when I'd gotten in trouble in high school. He'd spoken on my behalf at my hearing, and I had a feeling he was one of the reasons I hadn't gotten any jail time. After that, he'd started inviting me down here to the firehouse and giving me random jobs to do. He'd claimed he just needed the help, and at the time, I hadn't thought much about it. But he'd been looking out for me. Keeping me busy. Doing what he could to make sure I didn't screw up again.

"How's Evan?" he asked. "Home for the summer?"

"Yep, we're back to a full house."

"Things are about to get interesting around here. I got two new volunteer applications yesterday."

"Logan and Levi?"

He nodded.

"Good, I won't have to get on their cases to get them done."

I was glad Logan and Levi had finally graduated so they could apply to be volunteers, too. They were good guys, and thankfully they'd gotten through high school without any permanent damage. But it would be easier to keep an eye on them if they were here, especially since I was this close to pulling the trigger on getting my own place.

"Are you coming out for their graduation party?" I asked.

"Wouldn't miss it. Although I won't be staying late. I have to get on the road early the next morning."

"Going to visit Skylar?"

"Yeah, it's been too long since I've seen her. Couple more years and I'll be throwing her a graduation party. Or her mom will."

Unlike my parents, who'd been crazy enough to have five kids in less than six years, Chief Stanley only had one daughter. But he and his wife had divorced years ago, and Skylar lived with her mom about three hours away in Spokane. She didn't come out to Tilikum very often. I didn't know if that was her doing or her mom's, but Chief Stanley was usually the one to go to her. I hadn't seen her in years.

"Well, Gram managed to keep four out of the five of us alive until adulthood. Now she just has Gavin."

"God help her." He grinned. "He might be the toughest out of all of you."

I laughed. He wasn't wrong. Gavin seemed to have been born without the genes for fear. "I know. The kid's crazy."

"I'd say he'll grow out of it, but I doubt it. We just need to help him channel all that energy in the right direction. And who knows—maybe someday he'll meet a girl who mellows him out a little."

"Yeah, right."

"I've seen it happen. Remember, I knew your dad before he met your mom."

"Was he Gavin-level crazy? Because Gavin probably broke more bones than the rest of us combined by the time he was ten."

"He didn't have quite the same disregard for his mortality, but in a lot of ways, yeah, he was Gavin-level crazy."

I liked it when Chief Stanley talked about my parents. I almost never talked about them, but hearing bits and pieces of who'd they'd been, from someone who'd known them well, kept them alive for me in a way I appreciated.

I checked the time on the microwave, then started gathering my books into a pile. "I should get going. I have some stuff I need to do."

"All right. Have a good night. Say hi to Gram and the boys."

"I will."

I stuffed my books in my backpack and went down to my car, saying goodbye to some of the guys on my way out. A couple of them—Christian and Randy—were volunteers like me. Matt was the most recent permanent hire. They were good guys. We hung out sometimes outside of work hours, especially since I'd turned twenty-one and could go out for a beer with them.

Outside, it was hot, even for June. The mountain peaks stood out against the deep blue sky and the sun blazed. It wouldn't cool down until after sunset. I left my backpack in my car and walked the few blocks into town, heading for the coffee shop to meet Grace.

I hadn't made much progress with her—yet. She was set on going back to school in the fall, which I'd expected. She'd also said she didn't want a serious relationship, which I had to admit was a bit discouraging. I'd have to find a way to change her mind about that.

I understood where she was coming from. Although we'd basically grown up together, we'd had very different examples of relationships. Gram and Grandad had been the perfect couple—happy and completely devoted to each other. My parents had been good together, too. I remembered enough to know they'd been in love.

Grace had been raised by a single mom because her dad was a dick. It wouldn't have surprised me if the asshole was secretly married or something. Instead of growing up watching soulmates go through life together, she'd watched her dad screw over her mom. So I didn't blame her for being hesitant about the idea of getting serious with someone.

But I wasn't her father.

We'd hung out a few more times since we'd played pool at the Caboose, but somehow my brothers always managed to get in the way. A couple of days ago, I'd tried to take her on a hike out to a waterfall—if there was a good spot around here for a first kiss, that was it—but Gavin had seen us leaving. The next thing I knew, he'd grabbed Logan, and all four of us had gone hiking.

Last night we'd been in town and I'd suggested dinner. It was on the verge of being a date, but when we'd gone into the restaurant, Evan had been there. She'd felt bad that he was alone, so we'd had dinner with him.

Definitely not a date.

This afternoon wasn't going to be a date, either. But I did want to show her the apartment I was thinking about renting. Truthfully, I wanted her opinion in case it turned into *our* apartment.

And since I knew my brothers wouldn't be around to interrupt—they didn't know about the apartment yet—I'd use the opportunity to ask her out. It was going to mean taking things up a notch, but it was time I got a little more aggressive with her anyway.

I got to the Steaming Mug and went inside. The café was filled with the rich scent of coffee and a big chalkboard sign behind the counter advertised the menu. Grace and another girl were behind the counter, and the way Grace's face lit up with a smile when our eyes met fed my resolve.

Her hair was down today, and she took off her black apron. "Hey. Good timing, I was just finishing up."

"I can wait if you're not done."

"Nope, I'm ready." She turned to the other girl. "See you tomorrow?"

"Yep. I'll be here."

She disappeared into the back, then came out with her purse hanging from her shoulder. "Let's go."

I held the door for her and we started walking down the sidewalk. "How was work?"

"Not bad. It was busy when I got in this morning, but it calmed down this afternoon. Did you want some coffee before we go? I should have asked."

"No, although it smells good in there."

"Doesn't it? I love that little place. So where are we headed?"

"I want to show you something."

"Oh yeah? What is it?"

I glanced at her and grinned. "You'll see."

A man burst out of the alley between two buildings, nearly running into us. His thick beard and shaggy hair made his age hard to determine, although he had deep lines around his eyes. He blinked, looking around wildly, like he didn't know where he was.

"You okay, Harvey?" I asked.

His voice was gravelly. "What?"

"Were you going somewhere?"

He patted his well-worn clothes, like he was looking for something, sending puffs of dust into the air. Harvey Johnston lived just outside town, and had for as long as I could remember. He was a quirky old guy who dressed like a prospector from the gold rush, complete with a little pick that hung off his leather belt. I didn't know where he'd come from, or if he'd been this way his whole life. Maybe he'd suffered some kind of illness or accident. He wasn't exactly all there. He took care of himself okay, but sometimes he wandered around town, muttering about finding treasure in the mountains.

"Hey, Harvey," Grace said, trying to get his attention. "How are you today?"

He looked at her and his eyes finally seemed to focus. "Damn squirrels keep taking my walnuts."

"They do?"

"They're organized." He wagged a finger at her. "Organized, I tell you. Next thing ya know, they'll be goin' for my treasure too. Find it 'fore I do."

"I'm not sure if squirrels would be interested in treasure," she said. "They can't eat it."

His brow furrowed and he tapped his bearded chin. "True. Came into town for supplies. Me, not the squirrels. But I can't seem to—" He turned in a circle, then changed directions. "Where'd the store go?"

I grabbed his shoulders so he'd stop turning and pointed him in the right direction. "Straight that way, then take a left."

"A left? Yes, left. Good, good." He started shuffling up the street, still muttering.

"Think he'll get there okay?" Grace asked.

"Yeah, he'll find it."

We started walking again and I glanced behind me just in time to see Harvey take a left.

"I wonder if he'll ever find that treasure he's always talking about," she said.

"Not likely."

"You never know."

I glanced at her. "You think someone really buried treasure out there?"

"I'm just saying it wouldn't surprise me if crazy old

Harvey Johnston was actually onto something. Seems fitting for this town."

"Yeah, I suppose so."

Wrapped up in all the old stories about the origins of the town feud was the notion that someone had hidden something of value out in the mountains. People liked to call it buried treasure, but Gram had always brushed off the idea that it was a chest full of gold—although she didn't admit to knowing what it really was, or if anything was even out there. It was all a bunch of nonsense as far as I was concerned. The feud, the stories about buried treasure, all of it.

We turned down the next street, following the slope of the hill toward the river. I stopped in front of an old house that had been converted into two apartments, one upstairs, one down.

"Come on." I nodded toward the building and pulled the key out of my pocket. Herbert Bailey owned it and he'd let me borrow the key, even though I hadn't officially rented it yet. We were related, although I wasn't quite sure how. There were a lot of Baileys in Tilikum, so it was hard to keep track.

I unlocked the door and led Grace up the narrow wooden staircase to the second floor.

It was spacious for an apartment, with a living room, dining area, and a kitchen with maple cabinets. A short hallway led to two bedrooms and a bathroom. The walls were freshly painted and the carpet was new. Herbert had offered me a great deal—he'd called it the Bailey discount— which I appreciated.

She wandered to the center of the living room and turned in a slow circle. "Asher, is this..."

"I haven't signed a lease yet, but yeah. I'm getting my own place."

"Wow."

She kept looking around and I wasn't sure what that *wow* meant. Was she surprised? She couldn't think I'd live with Gram forever. Did she think it was a good idea? Was she imagining herself living here with me?

Probably not that last one, but I was working on it.

I followed her back to one of the bedrooms.

"This is big," she said.

"Yeah, but I can afford it."

"What made you decide to move out of Gram's house?"

I leaned against the door frame. "I just feel like it's time. I need my own space."

"I can understand that. Living with my mom after being away at school always feels like stepping back into childhood again." She gestured toward the other room. "Why two bedrooms? Are you going to get a roommate?"

Not if I can get you to move in with me sooner rather than later. "Not necessarily."

"Careful, or you'll end up with the twins as roommates."

"They're not invited."

She laughed and we went back to the living room. She wandered over to look out the large front window.

"So what do you think?" I asked.

"I like it. It's really nice."

"Yeah? I kind of wanted to see what you thought before I signed the lease."

Her smile faded and she fiddled with a strand of hair. She did that when she was nervous. "Oh. Well, yeah, it's cute."

Keeping my posture casual, I leaned against the half-wall in front of the stairs. It was hard not to blurt out that I was glad she liked it because I wanted to date her and hoped she'd eventually move in. That even though we were still young, I kind of wanted to fast-track things with her because I already knew she was it for me.

But what was I supposed to say? *Hey Grace, I'm pretty sure you're my soulmate, so what do you think about skipping ahead and just getting married?*

Yeah, no. That would be about as smart as kissing her in the middle of Gram's kitchen on her first day back would have been. And was I really thinking I'd marry her?

Yes. Yes, I was.

I knew she wasn't ready for that. But it was time to take the next step.

"So Grace, I was wondering—"

Her phone rang. "Sorry. Let me just check in case it's... Yeah, it's Mom. Hang on."

Damn it. "Yeah, sure."

She wandered toward the kitchen while she answered. "Hi, Mom... Yeah, I can pick him up... Of course... Don't feel bad, it's fine. I'll get us dinner. When do you think you'll be home?" She paused, listening. "Okay, see you then. Love you, too." She ended the call and dropped her phone back in her purse. "Sorry about that. Mom has to work late, so she needs me to pick up Elijah from the babysitter."

"Now?"

"Yeah. She was supposed to pick him up already, so I need to hurry."

"Do you need a ride?"

"No, I left my car over by the coffee shop. And I think I'll take him out for a cheeseburger on the way home."

I followed her down the stairs. "He'll love that."

"Yeah, he gets a little upset when she has to work late, so hopefully that'll help."

I locked the door behind us and fell in step with her as we walked back up the hill. I still wanted to ask her out, but now she seemed preoccupied. Worrying about her brother, probably. Naomi usually called Gram when she had to work late. It figured that she'd call Grace this time, right when I was about to ask her out on a date. Shitty timing.

She was parked in a small lot behind the coffee shop. We stopped next to her car.

"Thanks for showing me the apartment," she said. "It's exciting."

"Yeah, I think it'll be good. And I haven't told anyone else yet, so it would be great if you could keep it quiet for now."

She opened her car door and smiled. "No problem. It'll be our secret. I'll see you later."

"Bye, Grace."

Fingering the key in my pocket, I stepped back onto the sidewalk and watched her get in and drive away. I'd have other chances to ask her out. She lived right next door; it wasn't like it would be hard to see her. But I felt a little defeated. I'd built up that moment in my mind—imagined standing in that empty apartment and asking her out on our first date. Maybe getting bold and kissing her. It would have been cool to do it there.

But I wasn't about to give up.

7

GRACE

*S*omething was going on with Asher, and I wasn't sure what it was.

I stood outside in Gram's backyard with Logan and Levi's graduation party in full swing. The sun had already disappeared behind the mountain peaks, easing the heat of the day, and music from someone's stereo filled the air. It was crowded with family, friends, and neighbors. People balancing plates of food and drinks. Chatting and laughing. A bunch of people had even started dancing.

Levi and Gavin were testing the boundaries of the fire pit, building a blaze so high I was surprised Chief Stanley hadn't stopped them yet. Logan was walking around wearing his graduation cap, a Tilikum College t-shirt with the sleeves cut off, a pair of boxers instead of shorts, and white socks pulled up to his shins. Why? Who knew. It was Logan. He cracked jokes and ate up all the attention he was getting tonight.

If I had to guess, Levi was using bonfire-building as an excuse to avoid socializing with everyone, although I caught a few rare smiles from him as he and Gavin tossed more wood on the growing blaze.

Asher stood with Evan a few feet from the fire, a beer in his hand. His eyes flicked to me and his lips twitched with a hint of a smile.

He'd been giving me that look all day. I'd come over early to help set up, and no matter what we'd been doing— stringing lights around the porch, bringing out chairs, helping Gram in the kitchen—he'd been looking at me like that.

It was making me jumpy. He'd been touching me, too. Little nudges, or brushes of his arm against mine. Light touches on my lower back. He'd tugged my ponytail and when I'd smacked his arm for it, he'd winked at me.

If I hadn't known better, I'd have thought Asher had been flirting with me.

But this was Asher. He didn't flirt with me.

However, I couldn't shake the feeling that something was different. Gram would say the winds were changing, and that's exactly how it felt. Ever since Asher had come over to invite us for pie on my first day home, the feeling that things were different kept growing. Now, the air practically vibrated with it.

Elijah ran by with a cookie he'd probably swiped without asking. Or maybe Gram had slipped it to him. Either way, he wore a look of mischievous glee as he shoved it in his mouth. Gram herself sat in the old rocking chair on her porch, a contented smile on her face as she watched the party.

I walked up the porch steps and scooted a chair closer. She tipped slowly back and forth, her gentle cadence soothing as I sat next to her.

"Hi there, Gracie Bear." She reached over to squeeze my hand. "Thanks for the help earlier."

"Of course. It's a great party."

"The boys are happy. That's all I could ask for."

"I can't believe they graduated. It seems like the last few years have gone by so fast. First Asher, then me and Evan, now the twins. Next thing you know, it's going to be Gavin."

"Don't I know it. It won't be too long and I'll be living in this big old house all by myself."

I wondered if Asher had told her about the apartment yet.

And why had he told me first?

"Does that bother you? The idea of living here alone?"

She took a deep breath, still rocking gently. "Life is a series of seasons. Summer fades into autumn, but when the air gets cold and the leaves start turning, you always know summer will come around again. And you also know the next one won't be exactly like the last. It'll get hot, just like it does every year, but other things will have changed. I've had a long season of raising those boys and I'll miss it when it's over." She glanced at me. "But the next season of life will have its own blessings, and I look forward to those too."

I gazed at her for a long moment. "How did you get to be so wise?"

She chuckled. "A lot of years of living with my eyes open."

"As opposed to what, living with them closed?"

"Oh sure. Plenty of people go through life with their eyes squeezed shut. Most of 'em don't know any better. But they miss all the good stuff."

Asher glanced at me and his mouth turned up in that little grin again. Why did he keep doing that? There was heat in his eyes that sent a tingle down my spine.

I liked it.

And it was starting to scare me.

Because what if he *was* flirting with me?

There had been a moment in that empty apartment when a crazy thought had gone through my mind. That he was showing me because he thought we might live there together.

An unexpected spark of hope had flared to life. And then my mom had called, drawing me swiftly back to reality.

Now? I had no idea what to think.

A part of me clung to that bit of hope, refusing to let it fade away. Every smile, every wink, every touch from Asher fed it, keeping it alive.

But that hope was terrifying, because it meant rethinking everything. I was going back to school in the fall. Keeping my options for the future open, waiting to see where life would take me.

Was it leading me right back here?

A breeze picked up, making the sparks from the fire dance in a tiny whirlwind. The fresh night air brushed against my face.

Gram stopped rocking and leaned forward. She took a deep breath through her nose. "The winds are changing."

My eyes widened. "What?"

"That's the other thing about life and its seasons." She sat back and resumed her rocking, gently pushing the chair with her toes. "They don't always change when we think they should. Just when we're settling in to enjoy the crispness of autumn after the summer heat, we get an early snow."

My forehead creased and I looked over at her. She had her hands clasped in her lap and her long braid draped over one shoulder. Gram often said things that almost made sense, but left me wondering if I truly understood.

The noise in the spacious backyard grew. Logan had a girl hanging on him while he made a group of his friends laugh hysterically. Someone had started an ax-throwing contest in an open area down closer to the creek. Elijah was beelining for it, but Evan grabbed him, scooping him up onto his shoulders before he could get too close.

Even my mom looked like she was relaxed and having fun. She sat near the fire, chatting with Doris Tilburn. Her hair was down and she had a drink in a red plastic cup, a smile on her face. The number of people dancing grew, some pairing off as couples, others moving to the music in small groups around the fire.

Asher walked up the porch steps. He smiled, and the summer breeze stirred my hair.

"Hi, Bear," Gram said.

He leaned over and kissed her cheek. "How are you doing tonight, Gram?"

"My heart's full. It's good to have all my cubs in one place." She stopped rocking and pushed herself up out of the chair. "I think it's about time I made Logan dance with his Gram. He's lookin' a little big for his britches out there." She smoothed down her dress and glanced at me. "Keep your eyes open, Gracie Bear."

"I will." I wasn't sure what else to say.

I watched her make her way down to Logan. He said something into the girl's ear—she lived over on the other side of town, but I couldn't remember her name—then held out his arms for Gram. He led her closer to the fire and they started dancing.

Asher leaned against the porch railing. He wasn't

watching the party, or his brother dancing with Gram. He was watching me. "Hey, you."

A tingle of excitement made my heart flutter. "Hey."

"Wanna take a walk?"

"Sure."

He held out one of his strong, calloused hands to help me up, and the feel of his skin sent a buzz of electricity through me. Instead of moving back so I could go down the steps, he stayed where he was, just inches from me, his eyes intent on my face. He was so big. Asher's size was both imposing and captivating.

He was safe.

For the space of a heartbeat, I thought he might kiss me. But he just smiled—a slow, sexy grin that made my legs feel weak.

"Let's go."

He took my hand in his, clasping our fingers together. This time, he didn't tug me around the side of the house, joking that we had to sneak away. He held it like he meant it. Like this was important. Like *I* was important.

We walked down the porch steps and cut across Gram's land, heading for the road. The farther we got from the din of the party, the harder my heart beat. The moon was nearly full and the stars twinkled in their full glory away from the fire. We didn't need light to find our way. We'd grown up on this land. Getting lost would have been impossible.

Asher didn't say anything. Just held my hand while we walked. He didn't seem to be in any hurry, and I wondered if he had a destination in mind. Eventually we came to the road that led into town. He turned up it and we kept going, following the same route we'd taken to and from school countless times as kids.

The houses were closer together here. Some were dark

save for porch lights, their residents probably at Gram's house for the graduation party. Others had lights in the windows or the flicker of a TV peeking through the curtains.

Despite the way my heart raced with anticipation, being with Asher like this felt surprisingly natural. Our fingers fit together comfortably, like we'd done this a thousand times. Like we'd started dating back in high school instead of spending the last several years growing apart.

Something deep inside me ached for that version of reality. For a world where Asher and I were together. Because anything else felt so wrong.

That was an overwhelming thought to have while I walked hand in hand with him in the moonlight. To acknowledge how much my heart grieved for something I'd never had.

How could a few short weeks back home make me question everything?

It was Asher. *He* was making me question everything.

He stopped walking and I looked around in surprise. I hadn't been paying attention to where we were going. We stood in front of the old abandoned house on Evergreen Street. It was a ranch-style home, its big front window overgrown with blackberry bushes and ivy. A chimney hinted at a fireplace inside, but no one had lived here in years. The grass was waist high, and most of the property was choked with vines and thorny blackberries.

When Asher and I were kids, we'd often stopped in front of this old house on the way home from school. We'd made up stories about it being haunted, or played a version of "house," where he was the dad and I was the mom, and we were coming home from work. Once we'd even tried to break in, but everything had been locked up tight.

"Remember when we used to play house here?" he asked, finally breaking the long silence.

"Yeah, I was just thinking about that."

He was quiet again for a moment. We stood facing the house, still holding hands, the only sound frogs croaking somewhere nearby.

"I've had a lot on my mind lately." His voice was soft and low. "Growing up, and moving out, and the future. But I've also been thinking about the past. I feel like we went wrong somewhere, Grace. Like those kids we used to be were onto something."

My breath caught in my throat, and I wasn't sure what to say. So I waited.

"I made a big mistake in high school."

"What was that?"

"Not telling you how I felt about you."

I was grateful Asher didn't let go of my hand because the weight of his words nearly knocked me over. My voice came out in a whisper. "How did you feel about me?"

"The same way I do now." He turned me toward him and looked me in the eyes. "Grace, I'm in love with you."

I stared at him. At his dark brown eyes, his face silhouetted in the moonlight. At the man who'd been my best friend for most of my life. Who my heart had missed so much.

He ran his thumb across my lips. "It's okay; you don't have to say anything right now. I wasn't going to dump this on you tonight. I was only going to ask you out to dinner. I kept telling myself I had all summer to convince you to give us a shot and I needed to take it slow. But I just can't. I need you to know. I love you. I'm not asking you to say it back yet. All I'm asking for is a chance. Just give me the summer."

So many emotions swirled through me, I felt like bright

rainbows of feeling would burst from my fingertips. It was almost too much for my body to contain. "But Asher, I didn't think..."

"You didn't think I wanted you?" His eyes roved over my face and he traced his thumb down my cheek. "I've always wanted you. That was my mistake. I was afraid, so I never told you. I thought we were too close, that our families were too close, and if it didn't work out, I'd ruin things for everyone. But damn it, Grace, what if it does work out? What if this is everything I think it is?

"And I know you have school, and it's four hours away. But that's the thing—I'm not even worried about that. If we get to the end of summer and we want to stay together, we'll just do it long distance for a while. You can come home a little more often, and I can come see you in between. Plus, I only have one more year. After that, I could move to Pullman while you finish your degree. And then, I don't know, we decide where we want to be."

A tear broke free from the corner of one of my eyes, leaving a hot trail down my cheek.

He held my face in both hands and leaned down to rest his forehead against mine. "If the answer is no, I won't make things hard for you. I want you, but more than anything, I want you to be happy. I'm just asking for a chance."

He pulled away slightly and looked into my eyes. I stared back, captivated. He wasn't just a cute guy from college—someone who might be fun to hang out with. I couldn't date him casually, just to see where things went. He was asking for a summer, but if I gave him so much as a moment, I'd have to give him all my moments. My heart wouldn't accept anything less.

I didn't know how I could be so sure. How I could flip a

switch so quickly and be ready to change everything
for him.

Except this was Asher Bailey, and a part of me had
always known.

My answer left my lips on a whisper. "Okay. Yes."

"Yes?" His fingers slid through my hair, kneading my
scalp. "We'll start with dinner. Tomorrow?"

"Tomorrow is perfect." My eyes flicked to the house.
"And if things work out, maybe we'll wind up back here,
buying this old house to fix up together."

"Deal." He smiled, and emotion welled up in my chest,
tightening my throat. I'd seen Asher smile a million times,
but I'd never seen *this* smile. He was so happy, I could feel it.
As if our souls were intertwining and the depth of his
emotion flowed into me.

I'd give anything to keep seeing him smile at me like
this.

His hands were still in my hair, and his gaze dropped to
my mouth. Every nerve ending tingled with anticipation as
he drew closer, and I tilted my chin up to meet his kiss.

Our lips came together, his pressing against mine in a
gentle caress. My eyes drifted closed, and we hesitated there
for the space of a heartbeat.

With a subtle shift, he slanted his mouth over mine
more fully, and we sank into the kiss. I wound my arms
around his neck and parted my lips, inviting him in deeper.
His tongue slid against mine, warm and velvety soft.

The world around me fell away to nothing as he kissed
me deep and slow. I melted into him, surrendering. Secure
in his embrace. He was enticingly new and intimately famil-
iar, all at once.

He was everything. He was home.

8

ASHER

Whistling a random tune, I flipped the eggs over, silently congratulating myself when neither of the yolks broke. The scent of toast filled the kitchen and I wondered how long it would take for the smell of food to wake my brothers up.

Heavy footsteps pounded down the stairs. Not long, apparently.

"Morning," I said right as the toast popped up.

I heard the scrape of a chair, then Evan muttered a greeting. I plucked out the toast and tossed it onto a plate.

"Hungry?"

"Yeah, thanks."

Whistling again, I scraped some butter onto the toast, then slid the eggs on top. Perfect.

"You're in a good mood," he said.

I set the plate in front of him. Hell yes, I was in a good mood. How could I not be? I'd bared my soul to Grace—told her I loved her. And she'd agreed to give us a chance. "Yeah. So?"

"It's too early."

I went back to the toaster and dropped in two more slices of bread. "I was awake, so I figured I'd get up."

He scrubbed his hands over his face, then picked up his fork. "Me too. I had an early class last semester and now I can't sleep in. Where's Gram?"

I glanced out the window. "Out in the garden. Probably trying to do her thing out there before it gets too hot. Were you guys out late last night?"

"Yeah. After Gram went to bed, Logan and Levi and a bunch of their friends went down to the river. Gavin, too. I knew they'd have beer, so I went with them to make sure no one did anything stupid."

"Thanks, man." I felt kind of bad about that. Usually I was the one making sure our brothers got home in one piece. But by the time Grace and I had come back, the party had already broken up.

"It wasn't a big deal. No one got too crazy. Gavin jumped in the river with all his clothes on, but that's not new."

Chuckling, I cracked two more eggs into the pan. It was a running joke in our family that if there was water nearby, Gavin would get wet. When he'd been little, Gram had brought at least two changes of clothes for him wherever we went.

Now, she'd just shrug and tell him he was old enough to know how water worked.

I finished cooking my eggs, buttered my toast, and brought it all to the table. Evan had almost finished his breakfast, but he still didn't look awake.

I wondered if something else was bothering him. He tended to keep to himself, but he'd been extra quiet since coming home from school.

"You okay?"

He shrugged. "Yeah, just tired."

"Are you sure? It kinda seems like there's something going on." I folded a piece of toast around one of the eggs and took a bite.

He looked away, but instead of grumbling about needing more sleep or our brothers driving him nuts, his mouth turned up in a smile. "I sorta met a girl."

"No shit?" I paused, half-expecting Gram to scold me for my language even though she was outside. "Who is she? How'd you meet her?"

"Her name's Carly LiMarza. We were in a history class together last fall, but I didn't really talk to her until we wound up in the same study group for econ this semester. That was the early class. I probably would have dropped it, except she was in it."

I smiled and licked egg yolk off my fingers.

"Anyway, I finally quit dicking around and asked her out. Things have been going great, but she went home to California for the summer."

"And you miss her."

"It sounds stupid, but I'm basically counting down the days until we go back. We talked about getting together, maybe having her come up here, or me driving down there. But we both have to work all summer, so we decided to just suffer through. We've been Facetiming a lot."

"Why didn't you say anything? Does Gram know?"

"Yeah, I told Gram, but I didn't want to make a thing out of it yet. We've only been dating for a few months."

Evan was trying to play this off like it wasn't a big deal, but I knew him. And I recognized the look in his eyes. He was only twenty, but even though he was young, it wouldn't surprise me if he put a ring on that girl's finger sooner rather than later.

I just wondered which of us would do it first.

Probably me.

Thinking about rings made me think about Grace, which made me think about our date. And about kissing her last night. Her soft lips and my hands in her hair. I wanted to run next door and wake her up, just so I could kiss her again. I didn't want to wait until tonight.

I mopped up some egg yolk with my second piece of toast. Evan watched me with a furrowed brow.

"What?" I asked.

"Where were you last night?"

Grinning at him again, I took a bite.

"Ash."

"Grace and I went for a walk."

Grunting like he'd been hoping for a more interesting answer, he put the last piece of toast in his mouth.

"And I asked her out."

His eyebrows shot up his forehead and he swallowed almost without chewing. "You did what?"

"I asked her out on a date."

"Our Grace? Grace Miles?"

"Yeah."

"Why?"

"What do you mean *why*? Because I want to go out with her."

He stared at me for a few seconds, his brow furrowing. "Since when do you want to go out with Grace?"

"Since I do. You got a problem with that?"

"No, it's not a problem. I'm just surprised. She's..."

"She's what?"

"She's Grace. She's like our sister."

I scowled, like he was being gross, but I wasn't surprised he said that. I'd tried pretty hard to keep my feelings for

Grace to myself, and it had obviously worked. "She has *never* been like a sister to me."

"Who's never been like a sister?" Logan asked through a yawn. He shuffled into the kitchen, dressed in nothing but a pair of plaid pajama pants.

"Grace," I said. "Nice bedhead."

He raked his hands through his hair, messing it up even more. "I smell food."

I thought about telling him to make his own damn breakfast, but I was in a great mood, so why not. I got up and went to the fridge for more eggs. "Sit. I got it."

"Really? Awesome."

I put more bread in the toaster and kept the eggs out, since I was undoubtedly going to keep playing short-order cook when Levi and Gavin made it downstairs.

"Who's the girl you were with last night?" Evan asked.

Logan pulled out a chair and sat. "Which one?"

"The one you were making out with."

He grinned and scratched his head, making his hair worse. "Which one?"

I shook my head and cracked an egg into the pan.

"You're playing with fire, little brother," Evan said.

Logan just snickered.

More footsteps heralded the arrival of my last two brothers. Levi didn't say anything, just took a seat at the other end of the table. Gavin held a palm to his head, like he was in pain.

"What's wrong with you?" I asked.

"Shh." He winced. "Don't talk so loud. I think I hit my head last night."

"You didn't hit your head, dork, you drank too much," Logan said. "It's called a hangover."

"Seriously? This sucks."

"He shouldn't have been drinking anyway," Levi grumbled.

"It was just a few beers," Logan said. "He'll be fine. Drink some water, Gav."

Mumbling, Gavin got a glass of water and slumped into a chair. I kept cooking breakfast. The eggs started to sizzle, but they weren't quite ready to turn.

"What did you mean by that, Ash?" Logan asked.

"Mean by what?"

"That Grace has never been like a sister."

I could hear the suspicion in his voice. This was going to be interesting.

"Just what I said. You guys think of her as a sister. I don't. And..." I paused to flip the eggs. "I asked her out last night."

Logan flew to his feet. "Holy shit, Ash. You're going out with Grace? Wait, are you? Did she say yes?"

I glanced over my shoulder, at the four sets of brown eyes fixed on me. "Yeah, she said yes."

Logan smacked his hand on the table. "That's fucking amazing."

"Logan. Language." Gram's muffled voice came from outside.

He gaped at the back door—still closed. "How did she...?"

I plated Logan's food and set it on the table. "Look, I know this probably seems like it's coming out of left field. But you guys don't have anything to worry about. I'm serious about her."

"I don't think anyone doubts that," Levi said. "You don't need our permission to date her."

"You could have asked my permission," Gavin said. "What if I wanted to date her?"

Logan snorted. "You? Gavin, you're still in high school."

"So were you until like a month ago. And I won't always be in high school. She might have waited for me."

Logan patted him on the back. "I have some hard truths for you, buddy. Grace isn't going to wait for your balls to drop. And neither is Ms. Hanson."

My brow furrowed. "Who's Ms. Hanson?"

"Math teacher." Logan took a bite of his breakfast.

I shook my head again. Gavin had had crushes on every one of his babysitters from the time he was three, plus a handful of teachers over the years. The girls he actually dated were his own age, so I didn't worry too much about it. I tended to think he just wanted what he couldn't have.

"Hey," Gavin said, pointing at Logan. "Ms. Hanson is a beautiful, intelligent woman, and you never know what might happen after I graduate in a couple of years."

Levi rolled his eyes. "Gav, your math teacher is not going to date you."

Gavin scoffed. "You're just saying that because she wouldn't date you."

"I never—" Levi scowled. "Never mind. I'm not having this conversation with you."

"This sucks," Logan said around a bite of toast.

"Don't be a dick, Logan," Levi said. "Asher didn't have to make you eggs."

"No, the food is great," Logan said, gesturing to his plate. "But I can't make any inappropriate jokes about Asher going out with someone because it's Grace. Damn it, Ash, you always ruin my fun."

I laughed softly and went back to the stove to cook more eggs and toast. My brothers kept talking while I worked. The conversation moved on from me and Grace to Logan and Levi's training at the fire station and whether the wildfires would be bad this year. Then Evan told them about his girlfriend. Logan cracked a few jokes, Evan threatened to beat him senseless, and I couldn't help but feel like everything was right with the world.

By the time I handed Levi his breakfast, Gram was coming up the stairs onto the porch. The door let in a breath of fresh summer air before she clicked it closed behind her.

She paused next to the table and the lines around her eyes crinkled with her smile. "Breakfast time for my cubs, I see. You boys better clean up your own dishes."

She was met with a chorus of "We will" as she went to the sink to wash her hands.

Logan raised his eyebrows at me and mouthed, *Did you tell her?*

"Did he tell me what?" Gram asked without looking over.

"How does she do that?" he muttered.

I cleared my throat, preparing myself for a repeat of the *I thought she was like a sister to you* speech. "I asked Grace out on a date."

Gram turned off the water. "It's about time."

Her answer took me by surprise. "What?"

"Oh, come on now," she said. "I've been waiting for you to ask that girl out since you were sixteen. What took you so long?"

"You knew I liked her?"

"I have eyes, don't I?"

"They didn't know." I gestured to my brothers at the table.

She eyed them all like she wasn't impressed.

"Yeah, well, I'm taking her out tonight." My date with Grace wasn't the only big piece of news I had to share. I'd signed the lease on the apartment, but I still hadn't told them. "Gram, there's something else I need to tell you."

Her brown eyes were soft. "What's that, Bear?"

"I got an apartment in town."

My brothers all started talking at once.

"What?"

"You're moving out?"

"An apartment?"

"Where is it?"

"Boys." Gram hadn't raised her voice even a notch, but everyone quieted.

I continued. "It's on Timber Street, so it's walking distance to pretty much everything. Two bedroom—"

"Dibs," Logan said.

Levi groaned. "Damn it, Logan."

"I'll bunk with you, bro. It'll be like old times."

"Old times?" Levi asked. "We share a room now."

I let out an exasperated breath. "Neither of you are moving in."

"Then I get dibs," Gavin said.

"No."

"Why not?"

I turned to Gram, hoping she'd back me up, but she just smiled.

"Will you guys shut up so I can talk?" I paused for a second. "I'm moving out, *by myself*. I got a good deal on it, and I figured it was time. That's about it."

Gram squeezed my arm. "Big day for you."

"Yeah. It's not that I don't want to live here, I just—"

She put her hand up. "Bear, you're a man. Of course you're going to start your own life. It's how things should be."

"Thanks."

She squeezed my arm again. "I'm proud of you. Now, I have to run into town and then I'm meeting Mabel

Wheatley for lunch. If I don't see you later, have a nice time with Grace tonight."

"I will. Thanks."

"If there's a single dish in that sink when I get home, you're all sleeping outside." She headed for the stairs, but paused and glanced back at me. "You be a gentleman, Bear. And use protection."

I gaped at her in horror while my brothers snickered. "Gram!"

She didn't answer. Just chuckled and went upstairs.

The chairs scraped against the floor as my brothers all got up to clean their dishes. That hadn't been an idle threat; she really would make us sleep outside.

I cleaned the frying pan and wiped the breadcrumbs off the counter—still in a great mood. Things were coming together. I'd be moving my stuff into my new place in a few days. And tonight, I had a date with Grace.

A date I'd wanted for a long time.

9

GRACE

*S*tanding in front of the full-length mirror in the bathroom, I smoothed my dress over my hips. My college-student wardrobe didn't have much to offer in the way of date attire, so I'd gone into town and splurged on a new dress. It was black with thin straps and a straight neckline. A layer of sheer fabric on the outside added detail to the otherwise simple design. And I was showing a hell of a lot of leg. It was just long enough that I could sit down—but only just.

It was elegant and sophisticated—and different from anything I'd ever worn before.

I'd paired it with wedge-heeled sandals and painted my toenails bright red. My blond hair was down around my shoulders and I'd taken a gamble on some bold red lipstick.

I hardly recognized the woman staring back at me.

The doorbell rang, followed by Eli's feet thundering down the stairs. My heart fluttered. I'd never been so nervous in my entire life. Which seemed so silly. I didn't need to be worried about making a good impression, or whether we'd have anything to talk about. It was Asher.

But... it was Asher.

With a deep breath, I went downstairs to meet him for our first date.

He stood with Elijah and my mom just inside the front door, dressed in a button-down shirt with the sleeves cuffed and a pair of slacks. His gaze lifted to mine and a slow smile spread across his face. The same smile he'd given me last night—the one that shone from deep inside him, making my breath catch.

I was peripherally aware that my mom was smiling too. My brother stared at me like a stranger was walking down the stairs in his house.

"Why are your lips so red?" Eli asked.

"She's wearing lipstick," Mom answered.

"Why?"

Asher stepped forward, his eyes still locked on me. I let Mom field Eli's questions. I couldn't concentrate on anything but the man in front of me.

This wasn't *just* a date, any more than last night had been just a kiss. It felt like every road we'd taken had been leading us here, even when neither of us had known it. That he and I were as inevitable as the sunrise.

Before last night, I wouldn't have believed it. But the fact that the last twenty-four hours had changed the course of my entire life didn't seem the least bit strange. It wasn't rushed or shortsighted or reckless. It was right.

I was going to marry Asher Bailey someday.

Did he know it too? Was that what I could see in his eyes? We smiled at each other like we shared a secret. And maybe we did. Maybe that was our magic. We knew.

"You look beautiful." The hint of awe in his voice made my cheeks warm.

"Thank you."

He held his arm out for me and I tucked my hand in the crook of his elbow. "Ready?"

"Yeah."

"Have fun, you two," Mom said with a little wave.

We said goodbye amid Elijah's continued stream of questions. Asher led me out to his car and opened the door for me. I was practically giddy with excitement. I didn't know where we were going, but I didn't care. He could have been taking me to the Zany Zebra for greasy cheeseburgers and ice cream, and I would have been happy.

He took us to the south side of town, near the college, and parked outside a restaurant called Salt and Iron.

"Have you ever eaten here?" he asked as he helped me out of his car.

"No. It looks fancy."

"I haven't either. But I heard it's good."

His hand skimmed across my bare shoulder, down to the small of my back. He held the door and followed me inside.

Soft lighting illuminated an intimate space with dark hardwood floors and black-and-white artwork on the walls. About a dozen tables were adorned with white tablecloths and flickering candles. Quiet music played in the background, and only a few of the tables were full.

He'd made a reservation, and after he quietly conferred with the host, we were led to a table in the back. We both took our seats and the host handed us menus.

Asher eyed me for a second, then got up and moved to the chair beside me.

"What are you doing?"

"I like this better." His leg rested against mine and he slid his arm over the back of my chair.

I liked this better, too.

His fingers traced idle circles on my shoulder while we

looked at the menu. It was hard to concentrate on anything but the warmth of his body and the feel of his arm around me. When he asked if I knew what I wanted, he spoke softly near my ear, sending tingles running down my spine.

The server came to our table and we both ordered salmon, then chatted quietly while we waited for our food. With no one seated near us, it felt like we were tucked away —almost as if we were alone.

I liked that, too.

Our food arrived and Asher ate one-handed with his arm still draped behind me. I nestled in next to him, enjoying his closeness even more than my dinner. Which was saying something, because the food was amazing.

He asked me about school, and it didn't take long before I was telling him everything. About going to parties and sneaking into bars. About the friends I'd made. The whirlwind road trip we'd taken.

And I heard the details I'd missed from the last couple of years of his life. The first time he went on an emergency call. The guys from the fire station getting him drunk on his twenty-first birthday. The tournaments he'd won. What it was like having Evan gone during the school year.

Before this summer, our conversations had become shallow, barely skimming the surface. This was different, like we were catching each other up on all the important highlights of the last few years. Although we steered clear of the details of our dating lives. None of that mattered now, anyway.

We finished our dinners, but he didn't seem to be in any hurry to leave. I wasn't either. I was tucked up against him with his arm around me while he spoke softly near my ear. I could have stayed all night.

The server took our plates and told us to take our time. Asher paid the bill and thanked him.

"I can't remember if I mentioned it, but I'm competing in a jiujitsu tournament in a few days. Any chance you want to come?"

"Are you kidding? I'd love to."

He kissed my temple. "Awesome. I'd love to have you there."

"Of course I'll be there. Did you decide about the apartment?"

"Yep. I get the keys tomorrow."

"That's so exciting."

He nodded. "It's going to be different. Honestly, it's hard not to feel guilty."

"Guilty for what?"

"Not being there. I know I'll only be a few minutes away, but Gram's starting to slow down as she gets older. And the twins and Gavin are..."

"A handful," I said with a laugh.

"A big one."

"You know Gram can handle it. And like you said, you'll only be a few minutes away."

He brushed my hair off my shoulder. "I know. I'm probably worrying over nothing. I just didn't set the best example for my brothers when I was younger. I guess I feel responsible for them now."

"You weren't that bad."

He raised his eyebrows. "Grace, I probably spent more time in detention than in class."

"That's because you stopped hanging out with me." I poked him.

"You're not wrong. You would have kept me out of trouble. Or I would have gotten you into it."

I laughed. "Maybe."

He took a deep breath and glanced at the table, like he

was thinking. "Evan will be all right, as long as the girl he's dating is good for him."

"Evan has a girlfriend?"

"Yeah. He seems pretty into her."

"That's great."

"But then I look at Logan and the way he is with girls. And Gavin's complete disregard for his own mortality. And Levi still seems so angry."

I put my hand on his thigh. "You were pretty angry when you were eighteen."

He nodded slowly. "Yeah, I was."

I remembered that younger, angrier Asher, although he'd never taken it out on me. In fact, when we'd been alone, I'd seen a side of him not many people got to see.

"Well, maybe whatever helped you will help Levi, too."

"I hope something does. Maybe he just needs time to grow out of it."

"Is that what happened to you? You grew up?"

His fingers traced slow circles on my shoulder while he considered my question. "I think that's part of it. I also realized I had to step up and be a man, for Gram and my brothers."

"Why are you so amazing?"

He leaned closer and brushed his nose against my temple. "I'm not. I'm just doing my best." He paused again, taking a deep breath, like he was inhaling me. When he spoke again, his voice was quieter. "And I'm still angry sometimes."

I caressed his thigh. "About what?"

"That they're gone."

The sting of tears suddenly hit my eyes and I swallowed them back before they could fall. His parents. He almost never talked about them. The few times he'd tried when we were younger, he'd clammed up and either left or changed the subject.

"You miss them."

He rested his cheek against my temple and tightened his arm around me. "So much. It's been a long time, but sometimes it still really fucking hurts."

"I'm sorry," I whispered.

I shifted closer, wishing I could crawl into his lap. I wanted to wrap myself around him and hold him tight. It wasn't just that I wanted to make him feel better, although I did. I'd have done just about anything to soothe the pain he carried. But he was opening up to me. As close as we'd been as kids, I'd never felt as connected to him as I did right now.

He pressed his lips to the side of my forehead and trailed his fingers through my hair.

"I know it's not the same because my parents are alive, but I'm angry sometimes, too. At my dad."

"No shit. I'm angry at your dad, too."

I laughed softly, but there was a hint of a menacing growl in his voice that was a little bit scary. Not that I could ever be afraid of him, but I wondered what would happen if he ever got his hands on my dad. As much as I hated my father, I decided I didn't want to know.

"I'm more concerned for Elijah than myself. I know what my dad's like, and I don't expect anything from him. But it won't be long and Eli's going to start wondering why he doesn't have a dad at home. Or at least one who visits him."

"It won't be easy. But he's going to turn out okay."

"Yeah, he's a good kid. My mom does her best, and he has Gram, and all of you."

"Hopefully our influence on him is more good than bad, although I can't promise anything."

I laughed again.

He brushed his fingers down my neck and across my shoulder. "I'm not overwhelming you, am I?"

"No, not at all."

"Are you sure? I can't stop touching you. I'm trying not to be inappropriate, but I have to be honest, it isn't easy. You look incredible. And don't even get me started on how good you smell." He put his face in my hair and inhaled.

I turned, lifting my chin so my face was in his neck, and breathed him in. His warm, woodsy scent sent a cascade of sensations through my entire body. "You smell good, too."

A low groan rumbled in his throat. "We should probably go. I need to kiss you like I need to breathe, but I don't want to get us kicked out."

We stood and he took my hand in his, then led me out to his car. But instead of opening the door for me, he pushed me up against it and captured my lips with his. My hands slid up his broad chest and I draped my arms around his shoulders, melting into his kiss.

I wasn't sure how long we stood there. Probably only a few minutes, but time ceased to have meaning when Asher was kissing me. Eventually, we got in his car and drove home.

He parked outside my mom's house and turned off the engine. Leaning over, he kissed me again.

"Thank you," I said. "Tonight was perfect."

His mouth hooked in a grin. "Really?"

"It was the best date I've ever had."

"Does that mean I get another one?"

Another one... a lifetime of them. "Definitely. And Asher?"

"Yeah?"

I reached over to clasp his hand. "Remember what you said last night?"

"I said a lot of things."

"I know. But one of them stands out. You said you were in love with me."

His voice was quiet. "Yeah. I did."

"I'm in love with you, too."

He let out a breath and there was both relief and happiness in his smile. "Oh my god, I can't even tell you how good it feels to hear you say that."

"I've always been in love with you. I just didn't think you could love me back, so I—"

He cut me off with a kiss.

We probably had an audience, but I didn't care. I kissed him in the moonlight, lost in the feel of his mouth tangled with mine.

Amazed that this was really happening.

10

GRACE

*T*he huge gym buzzed with energy, and the scent of buttery popcorn drifted in from the hallway. Sets of tall bleachers surrounded the mats, and teams of jiujitsu competitors in matching gis clustered in groups along the sidelines.

Asher had told me what to expect. Eight mats in two rows of four. There would be matches held on each, simultaneously. The far left were for the female divisions. His matches would probably be on the right, so I picked my way through the crowd and found a seat.

I'd seen Asher compete in sports in high school—been to football games and wrestling matches. But I'd never been to one of his jiujitsu tournaments. I was surprisingly nervous.

The bleachers were hard and many of the spectators had brought cushions to sit on. I'd probably be wishing I had one of those before too long.

Asher and his team gathered around their coach. They each wore a white gi, belted at the waist, with the gym logo on the back. Levi and Logan were there too, looking more alike than usual with their matching serious expressions. Gavin was with them but dressed in street clothes; he had a minor injury and wouldn't be able to compete today.

According to Asher, he'd fought the coach so hard on that point, he'd almost been temporarily suspended from the team. Fortunately, Asher had talked some sense into him before he got himself into too much trouble.

I watched while Asher led his teammates in a warm-up. He looked calm, totally in his element. His eyes swept the crowd a few times while he stretched, finally finding mine. He gave me a quick wink, sending a tingle of excitement fluttering through my tummy.

Our transition from friends to lovers had been fast, but seamless. Like it had been inevitable all along. And now that we were dating, I didn't have to hide the way I looked at him. I could watch him with undisguised desire, knowing that man out there was mine.

It was a heady thought. I chewed my bottom lip while little sparks of arousal warmed me from the inside.

Asher had warned me there was a lot of waiting at tournaments, and he wasn't wrong. But eventually the mats cleared, and a man in a button-down shirt welcomed the crowd and announced the start of the tournament. The matches began with the lightest weight classes; Asher would be a while.

Even though I didn't know who most of the competitors were, the initial matches were fascinating. Jiujitsu didn't involve striking moves, like punching or kicking. Asher trained in that kind of fighting too, but today was all grappling. Competitors won either by scoring points for executing moves or by putting their opponent in a submission hold.

I was glad this was just grappling, not MMA fighting. I'd

seen Asher after sparring at his gym, and he'd come away with cuts and bruises more than once. He'd always shrugged off the injuries as minor, but I didn't particularly want to watch someone trying to punch him.

Still, the submissions looked painful.

I could have sworn one guy was about to dislocate his opponent's shoulder. Another got caught in a choke hold that had his entire face turning purple before he tapped out. I found myself caught up in the excitement of the competition, cheering for Asher's teammates when it was their turn. Shouting encouragement and clapping at the end, regardless of the winner.

In between matches, I scanned the other teams, wondering who'd be going up against Asher. There were quite a few men who appeared similar in size. One paced back and forth on the other side of the gym, his eyes locked on Asher. His head was buzzed and even though he wore a dark blue gi, there was no mistaking the muscle underneath.

Asher watched him too, like a wolf tracking a potential rival. There was no hostility in his gaze. Just focus. He exuded composure—a confidence that, to me, seemed far more intimidating than the intense glares he was getting from the guy in blue.

Levi won his first match in less than thirty seconds, earning an enthusiastic response from the crowd. Logan grappled after him, and although his match lasted longer, he made his opponent tap out. Both returned to the sidelines to high fives and pats on the backs from their teammates.

Finally, it was Asher's first match. His first opponent was a man in a black gi from a gym in a neighboring town, not the guy in blue. It was over almost before it began. One minute the ref was blowing the whistle and both men were on their feet. The next, Asher had him on the ground, twisted into a position that looked like it hurt. The guy in black tapped out, the whistle blew again, and it was over.

Asher helped the other guy to his feet, and they shook hands. Then the ref raised Asher's arm, declaring him the winner. I jumped up, clapping and cheering for him. A few people shot me annoyed looks, but I didn't care. I was going to cheer for my man.

The wait for his second match wasn't long. This one went the full round, and by the end, my heart was hammering in my chest and I'd left fingernail prints in my palms from clenching my fists so hard. I didn't understand exactly how the scoring worked, but Asher had won on points. The ref lifted his arm and I cheered my heart out again.

He stayed with his teammates, but met my eyes often, offering a wink or a half-smile. When Levi and Logan were up, he helped coach each of them through their next matches. Both won, moving on to the next round.

So did the guy in dark blue.

The tension in the gym grew as the afternoon went on and more competitors were eliminated. My butt hurt from the hard bleachers, but as Asher walked out onto the mat for his final match, all thoughts of discomfort fled.

Because of course he was up against the guy in dark blue.

They nodded to each other with what looked like respect. I didn't know who he was, but I had a feeling he and Asher had competed against each other before. They were similar in height and build—both tall and athletic—and both moved with a similar confident grace.

My eyes were locked on them, my heart in my throat.

They shook hands, stepped back, and the ref blew the whistle.

I watched in awe as the two men fought to take each other down. Within seconds it was clear they were evenly matched. This wouldn't be an easy win for either of them.

Asher moved with stunning power and speed, finally gaining the upper hand. He hooked his opponent's leg and the next thing I knew, they were on the mat.

From there, it was hard to tell who was winning. My heart raced and I clenched my fists, leaning forward as I watched the battle. Asher strained against his opponent, his face intense. I was close enough to hear his low grunts as they fought—and my god, it was ridiculously arousing.

I'd never seen this side of Asher before. He was so focused and there was so much ferocity in the way he moved. He was powerful and strong, with a hint of anger in his expression and danger in his dark eyes.

If I hadn't known him so well, it might have scared me a little.

His brothers shouted encouragement from the sideline and his coach barked instructions. The crowd cheered, the noise thick around me. Sweat dripped down Asher's temples and his opponent's face was flushed bright red.

"Come on, Asher!" I had no idea if he could hear me, but I yelled a steady stream of encouragement as the two men fought for dominance.

The guy in blue got Asher on his back and I gasped. But Asher locked his legs around him, pulled him down closer, and hooked a leg across his neck. Suddenly, he had his opponent's head and one arm trapped with his legs.

Asher's jaw clenched tight as he held the position. The other guy tried to break free, but his already red face quickly deepened to a dark purple. A few seconds later, he tapped Asher's leg with his free hand.

It was over. Asher had won.

I shot to my feet, clapping like a crazy person. The guy in blue stood first and reached a hand down to help Asher up. They spoke and I could see the mutual respect as they shook hands again.

Then the ref lifted Asher's arm and the crowd cheered.

My cheeks felt flushed and my heart beat fast. Asher came straight for me, and I scrambled down from the bleachers to meet him. I launched myself at him, throwing my arms around his neck. He picked me up off my feet and squeezed me tight.

"That was amazing," I said in his ear. "You were so incredible."

"Thanks, baby," he said, still breathing hard. "Thanks for being here."

"I'll always be here for you," I said. "Always."

11

ASHER

My apartment was still mostly empty. I'd bought a bed, so at least I had a place to sleep. And between a box of kitchen supplies Gram had brought over and a shopping trip with Grace, I had everything I needed to be functional.

Except furniture. But aside from the bed, that was going to have to wait.

I'd saved a little money, intending to use it for the basics —a couch and a table at least. But after that first date with Grace, I'd scrapped my plans. I had something more important to buy.

I hadn't bought it right away, although that had been a function of being busy as much as anything. I had to work, go to the gym, take my shifts at the firehouse. In between, I spent almost every spare moment with Grace.

But as soon as I'd gotten off work today, I'd done it. And now instead of a furnished apartment, I had a little box with Grace's engagement ring.

I wasn't sure when I was going to ask her. I didn't want to rush her, and we'd only been dating for about a month.

Which was kind of a mind fuck, because it felt like we'd always been together. Like those years of drifting apart hadn't really happened.

Still, I didn't want to get the timing wrong. And simply having the ring felt good. I'd taken another step toward our future. My plans were coming together.

I put the box away, tucking it up on a shelf in my bedroom closet. It would be there when we were ready.

Grace was probably home from work by now, so I left to go pick her up, locking the door behind me. Living alone was different, but I liked it. It felt good to have my own space.

I still saw my family all the time. Logan and Levi were in training to be volunteers, so they were at the firehouse a lot. Gavin seemed to find his way down there on a regular basis, hanging around like I had when I was younger. And Gram had instituted Tuesday dinners, insisting that no matter what happened in our lives, if we were within driving distance, we were expected to be there.

Grace also joined us. Every week.

It hadn't taken long for both of our families to get used to me and Grace being together. My brothers groaned and complained when I kissed her in front of them, telling us to get a room. Gram remained completely unsurprised that we'd started dating and I was pretty sure she suspected I'd buy a ring—probably soon.

Even Naomi was happy for us. I hadn't been sure how she'd feel about me dating her daughter. Grace wasn't much older than Naomi had been when she'd gotten pregnant, and I didn't want her to worry that I'd turn Grace's life sideways. When I went over to pick up Grace for our second date, I'd told Naomi, straight up, that I loved her daughter and I wasn't going anywhere. She'd hugged me and simply said, "I know."

Grace came outside as soon as I pulled up in front of her house. She looked adorable in a t-shirt and cut-offs, with her hair up and her purse slung over her shoulder. I got out of my car as she bounded down the steps, and she practically jumped into my arms. I kissed her, reveling in the sweet relief of her lips.

"Hi, beautiful."

"Hi." Her arms tightened around my neck and I squeezed her back. "I missed you today."

"I missed you, too." I held her for a long moment, just enjoying the feel of her against me. "What do you want to do tonight? Are you hungry?"

She pulled away. "You know, I'm really not. I had a late lunch. But if you are…"

"Actually, I'm not either."

"Okay." She caught her bottom lip between her teeth and something about the look in her eyes stirred a hot sense of need inside me.

So far, we'd waited. We'd made out—a lot—but we hadn't slept together. I didn't want to rush her when it came to that either, but fuck, I wanted her. And the way she was looking at me with undisguised desire in her eyes made me want to drag her back to my apartment like a caveman.

Come on, Asher. Be a gentleman.

"I was thinking…" She licked her lips and a hint of pink crept across her cheeks. "Maybe we could go hang out at your place tonight."

We almost never hung out at my place. There wasn't any furniture, and not much to do. No TV or anything. So why would she…

Oh shit, did she mean…?

"Yeah, sure, if you want. Although the only furniture I have is the bed."

"I know."

Before I could stop myself, a low groan rumbled in my throat, and I pulled her close. The kiss I gave her was downright obscene, considering we were standing in front of both of our families' houses, and chances were good we had an audience. But I didn't care. I invaded her mouth with my tongue and pressed my very solid erection against her.

"Is that what you want, beautiful?"

Her hand slid down and briefly skimmed over my cock through my pants. "Yes."

"Let's go."

We got in my car and I clasped her hand in mine. Brought it to my lips for a kiss a few times on the way to my place.

My body buzzed with anticipation as I walked her to my door. The tension between us was palpable, making my heart thump in my chest.

I unlocked the door to let us in, then held her hand on the way up the stairs. I hesitated at the top, but she gently tugged my hand in the direction of my bedroom.

That was all the encouragement I needed. I took the lead, pulling her down the short hallway into my room, and kicked the door closed.

Sliding my fingers through her hair, I tasted her lips. Lapped my tongue against hers, hungrily licking into her mouth. Her hands slipped beneath my shirt and her palms splayed across my skin.

Still kissing her, I guided her to the bed. She lay down and I climbed on top of her. We were still dressed, but as much as I ached for her—and as hard as it was getting to actually think—there was something I needed to say before I got her naked.

I brushed her hair back from her face. "Grace, I kind of need to tell you something."

"I do, too. But you first."

"I haven't..." I hesitated, not sure how to say this. I'd never told anyone. "I've never actually done this. At least, not all of it."

Her lips parted. "You haven't?"

"No. I've done... other stuff. And I tried a couple of times, but I stopped it before it got that far. Don't get me wrong, I *can*. Everything works." I ground my erection into her a little, just to prove my point. "It just never felt right."

She touched the side of my face. "Oh, Asher."

"Maybe I'm old-fashioned, but I've never been able to separate sex and love. And you're the only woman I've ever loved."

Her eyes held mine and her smile lit up her face. "I haven't either."

"Really?"

"No. I've never wanted to with anyone else."

"Oh my god, I love you so much." I kissed her again, instinctively rolling my hips.

Her soft moan into my mouth set me on fire.

But just because I hadn't had sex before didn't mean I was going to be a bumbling idiot about it. I took my time undressing her, caressing and kissing her skin. Touching her. Exploring. And letting her explore me.

I rolled onto my back and took my pants off. Our shirts were long gone, and she was down to nothing but a lacy pink bra and matching panties. She propped herself up alongside me and skimmed her hand over my chest, down

my abs, toward my hard length. My muscles tensed in anticipation.

She met my gaze and raised her eyebrows. I grinned at
her. *Yes, Grace, you can definitely touch my cock.*

Her fingers brushed the tip and I sucked in a quick
breath.

"Is that okay?"

"Definitely okay." There was a hint of strain in my voice.
"Take your time."

She touched me again, her fingers gliding down the
shaft, then up again. I watched, fascinated, as her confidence increased. She wrapped her hand around me and
gently squeezed.

I groaned, my eyes rolling back.

"I want to know what feels good," she said.

"Fuck, Grace, right now everything feels good." I
reached down and put my hand around hers. "You can
squeeze harder."

Her voice was breathy. "Okay."

She tightened her grip, and I grunted at the increased
pressure.

"What else?"

"You can stroke it, like this." I guided her hand up and
down my cock. I had to be careful, or she was going to make
me come way too soon. Something about her hand and my
hand both moving up and down the length of my erection
was unbelievably hot.

Still, there was so much of Grace I hadn't explored yet. I
rolled to my side, nudging her onto her back. "Can I touch
you too?"

Biting her lip, she nodded.

I helped her out of her bra and panties and tossed them
to the side. Her tits were round, her nipples pink. And god,

the way her waist curved into her hips.

"Holy shit, Grace. You're so beautiful."

She smiled at me, nibbling on her bottom lip again.

Leaning down to kiss her, I cupped one of her tits, then ran my thumb over her nipple. I stroked it a few times, teasing it into a hard peak. She moaned when I took it in my mouth and sucked gently.

"Does that feel good?" I asked.

"Yes. So good."

I traced my hand down her body, pausing at the apex of her thighs to make sure she was comfortable. She tipped her legs open, inviting me in.

Softly kissing her lips, I let my fingers explore. I traced her slit, then dipped a single fingertip inside her. She was temptingly warm and wet.

"More?"

"Yes."

I slid my finger in deeper—slowly, carefully. Learning the way she felt. What made her hips jerk and moans escape her lips. "Show me where it feels good."

She reached down and placed her hand over mine. Together, we found her clit, and she showed me how to touch her. First one finger inside her, then two. She guided me in a steady rhythm, my fingers in her pussy, the pad of my hand rubbing her clit.

I watched in awe as her inhibitions fell away. Her body moved, her hips tilting in time with my strokes. Lips parted, cheeks flushing, breath coming fast. Her legs fell open wider and her eyelids fluttered. I moved faster, her hand still on top of mine, and her walls tightened around my fingers.

"Oh god, Asher," she breathed.

Fuck, yes. I fingered her faster. Harder. Her moans were

rhythmic and desperate, her hips bucking against my hand. I flicked her nipple with my tongue and she cried out.

Her back arched, her grip on my hand tightened, and her pussy spasmed around my fingers. She squeezed her inner muscles, rolling her hips with the pulses of her orgasm.

Watching her come made my heart pound and my dick throb. She was so fucking sexy.

And so fucking wet.

Her climax subsided and I slid my fingers out. I kissed her and she draped her arms around me while her body relaxed against the sheets.

"How did that feel?"

"So good."

"Grace, I want to be inside you. Are you ready for that?"

"Yes. I'm so ready."

I rolled over to get a condom out of the crate I was using as a nightstand. I hadn't been sure when I would need them, but right now I was really glad I'd decided to be prepared.

After rolling the condom on, I climbed on top of her. My cock nudged at her opening. But as much as I wanted to be inside her, I didn't want to hurt her.

"Tell me if this hurts too much, okay?"

She nodded.

I held her gaze as I gently pushed inside her. Slow. Painfully slow. The instinct to drive into her and fuck her senseless was strong, but I kept my head. She gasped and a flicker of pain crossed her face.

"Are you okay?"

"It hurts a little, but I really don't want you to stop."

I kept going, stretching her open. Feeling her wrap around me. She was hot and tight around my cock, and nothing—*nothing*—could have prepared me for how incredible she felt.

Careful not to move too fast, I pulled out slightly, then pushed back in. She tensed, but slid her hands down to my lower back. I moved out, then in again, with the pressure of her hands guiding me. Gradually, I felt her body relax. Felt her legs open wider and her hips roll against me.

Her hands pressed into my back each time I thrust inside her. I let her body, and my instincts, show me what to do. The more she relaxed, the faster I moved, and the deeper I drove into her.

"Are you good?"

"Yes. Don't stop, you feel amazing."

I plunged into her, grunting with every thrust. The pressure in my groin built fast. I was surrounded by her. By the softness of her skin, sliding against mine. By her scent in my nose. Her taste on my lips. I kissed and licked her, lapping my tongue against her neck. Driving my cock in and out of her wetness while she moaned and murmured in my ear.

Growling, I fucked her harder. Deeper. She dug her fingers into my back and drew her knees up. My muscles flexed, my hips jerking against her. She felt so good, it was unreal. I thrust in again and my entire body clenched tight.

And I came undone.

With white hot pulses, I came inside her. I groaned, the intensity overwhelming. She clung tightly to me while I rode out the waves of my orgasm, still thrusting deep.

When I finished, I gently pulled out. I was breathing hard and could barely think, but I climbed off her to deal with the condom. Leaving it tied off by the bed—and making a mental note to get a trash can in here—I turned and gathered her in my arms.

We lay there together for long moments, just breathing.

I was warm and sated in a way I'd never felt before. My body was content, but—more than that—so was my soul.

I kissed her head and she nestled in closer. Although I'd kept my sexual status to myself—it wasn't anyone else's business—I hadn't felt bad about it. I'd just wondered what it was going to take for it to feel right.

Now I knew. And if I'd had even the slightest trace of regret at not having slept with a woman yet, it was gone. I hadn't intended to wait for Grace, but I was so glad I had.

So fucking glad.

I didn't care what other people would think or say about a guy who was only with one woman his whole life. This was what I wanted. Just her.

She was my first love, even though I'd taken too long to tell her. And she was going to be my only love. I knew that now more than ever. Grace was it for me.

12

GRACE

*A*sher had asked for a summer—a chance to show me that we'd be good together. Not that I'd needed any convincing. From the moment he'd kissed me outside the old house on Evergreen Street, I'd been his. And I'd known it could never be just a summer. Not when it was us.

So when summer ended, I stayed.

The deadline to apply as a transfer student to Tilikum College had already passed, so I decided to take a year off instead of going back to WSU. Asher argued with me about it, but I'd made up my mind. I wasn't leaving. After all, it was only a year. Most of my scholarships allowed for a break, so I'd be able to pick up next fall where I left off. And I'd miss the friends I'd made, but we'd keep in touch.

Once I convinced Asher that I was doing the right thing, we spent the rest of the night celebrating. Naked, of course.

Not that we ever needed a reason to get naked. We were insatiable.

My mom's reaction to my decision to stay surprised me. I was prepared for her to try to talk me out of it. She'd been so adamant I go away to school and follow my dreams. But she didn't. In fact, she tearfully admitted she was relieved. Raising a little boy on her own was tough. She'd never wanted to put pressure on me to stay for her sake, but she was glad that I'd be here.

That, more than anything, made me decide to live with her for the time being. Asher had asked me to move in with him, and I would—probably sooner rather than later. But I told him I thought I should stay with my mom for a while— that she needed me.

He understood. He felt a responsibility to his family, too. We had that in common.

And the funny thing was, my old bedroom didn't feel like it was trying to drag me back in time anymore. It was just a room—a place to sleep and keep my things. Maybe the difference was that I'd made a choice. I wasn't living there by default, stuck in stasis while I waited for my life to move forward. Now I had a clear vision of my future, and this was merely one step along the way.

Summer turned to fall, the multicolored leaves transforming our little mountain town into a riot of oranges, reds, and browns. Evan went back to school. Elijah turned four and we threw him a firefighter birthday party. Gavin grumbled about still being in high school, and Levi and Logan started college. Logan even behaved himself. Mostly.

Asher and I fell into a comfortable routine. We both had jobs, and he had classes and shifts at the fire station. Otherwise, we were together. We spent lazy days in his apartment, tangled in his sheets. He took me out on dates—to the movies, or dinner, or to play pool at the Caboose. We hung out with friends, or his brothers. And every Tuesday we had dinner at Gram's house.

The snows came early, blanketing everything in white. We recreated childhood memories with snowball fights—

although now they ended with cozy make-out sessions to warm up, instead of hot chocolate in Gram's kitchen.

We did a bar crawl on my twenty-first birthday. Spent Christmas together with both of our families. We rescued Logan and Gavin when they got their grandad's old truck stuck in the snow on a dirt road just outside town. Took Levi with us on a road trip to see Evan.

And it was hard to imagine life getting better.

Until it did.

~

I WOKE up in Asher's bed to the sound of the shower. I'd slept over, and my body was still pleasantly sated from all the things he'd done to me last night. Arching my back, I reached my hands over my head in a lazy stretch. We both had the day off from work, but Asher had class, and my mom needed me to pick up Elijah and watch him for a few hours.

The water turned off. I stayed in bed, waiting for him to finish in the bathroom. A few minutes later he came in with damp hair and a towel wrapped around his waist.

He grinned at me and let the towel drop. "Morning."

"Morning." I enjoyed the view while he rubbed the towel over his hair a few times, then grabbed his clothes. There were certainly benefits to being with a man who kept himself in such good shape. The tattoos on his arm highlighted the ripples of muscle. His thighs were thick and sturdy, and his ass... God. I wanted to bite right into it.

"Hey, can you meet me at the firehouse this afternoon?" He finished pulling on his jeans and buttoned them. "I'm heading over there after class."

I kind of wished we could just stay in bed together all

day, but meeting him later would have to do. "Yeah, I can do that. I'll text you when I get there."

He tugged a t-shirt over his head. "Awesome." Pausing next to the bed, he eyed me for a second. "Damn it, you look so good, I could fuck you again right now. But I can't be late."

I reached for him and he leaned down to kiss me. "It's okay, I'll be more than happy for you to fuck me again later."

With a smile, he kissed me again. "Perfect. I'll see you this afternoon?"

"Yep."

He kissed me a few more times, then groaned, like he was reluctant to leave. Finally, we said goodbye, and I got up to shower.

I spent the morning running a few errands, then picked up the mail for my mom when I got home. I noticed an envelope from my father among the bills and junk mail. It looked like it had a check in it, which was a damned good thing. I'd have been pissed if it didn't.

Elijah got out of his preschool class at noon, so I picked him up and took him home. He babbled about using tissue paper and glue to make an art project and how they had string cheese and fish crackers for snack time. I fed him lunch and set him up at the table with crayons and a new coloring book Asher had picked up for him the other day. When he got tired of that, I let him watch cartoons while I started dinner so my mom wouldn't have to cook tonight.

Mom came home from work looking tired. I made us both some tea, then we sat at the table and chatted for a while. Getting off her feet seemed to help perk her up.

"Are you staying for dinner tonight?" she asked.

"No, I'm supposed to meet Asher."

"That's fine. I need to run to the store first, but I'll take

Eli with me so you can go." She stood and took our mugs to the sink. "Get your shoes on, buddy. Wait, go potty first."

He groaned. "I don't have to."

"Go try anyway."

He got up with a sigh and shuffled to the bathroom.

Mom shook her head. "You never argued about going to the bathroom when you were little. I wonder if it's a boy thing. Maybe I'll ask Gram."

"She would certainly know."

"Yeah she would. I swear, that woman is a saint, raising five grandsons."

"She is pretty amazing. But so are you."

She smiled. "Thanks, honey. And thanks for everything today."

"It's no problem."

Elijah came out and put on his shoes and coat while Mom put the casserole I'd started in the fridge so she could heat it up when they got back. I said goodbye, but didn't leave to meet Asher yet. I hung back so I could clean up a little and run a load of dishes. I knew my mom would appreciate coming home to a tidy house.

After I finished, I drove into town and parked at the fire station. The snow had mostly melted and the spring air smelled fresh. I paused outside my car to send Asher a text, letting him know I was here. My stomach fluttered with anticipation. Which seemed a little silly, considering I'd been with him this morning. But I couldn't wait to see him.

Harvey Johnston sat on a bench in the big grassy area outside the station. Asher replied that he'd be out in a minute, so I wandered over to say hi.

He stood and tipped his hat to me. "Afternoon, Miss Grace."

"Hi, Harvey. How are you today?"

"Okay. Except those damn squirrels stole my ax."

I raised my eyebrows. The squirrels around here were routinely blamed for things going missing, but an ax? "Really? How big was it?"

He used his hands to indicate what seemed like a normal-sized ax. "'Bout like that."

"That must have been pretty heavy. Do you think a squirrel could lift it?"

"Not *a* squirrel." He raised a finger. "But they're organized."

"Why do you think they took it?"

He narrowed his eyes. "That's what I'm trying to find out."

"Oh, okay. Well, I hope you find it. Or that the squirrels return it."

"They will if they know what's good for 'em."

"Hey, beautiful."

I turned at Asher's voice, a smile already on my face. "Hey."

He slipped a hand around my waist and placed a light kiss on my lips. "I missed you today."

"I missed you, too."

"You better marry that girl, Bailey," Harvey said.

Asher laughed. "You think so?"

Harvey nodded gravely and his eyes were surprisingly clear. "Yes."

"Thanks, Harvey. I'll keep that in mind." He winked at me. "I need to grab something before we go. Come with me?"

"Okay, sure." I turned to Harvey. "Bye, Harvey. I hope you find your ax."

He tipped his hat to me again. "Bye. Ax, right. Gotta find it. Damn squirrels."

Asher put his hand on the small of my back and led me toward the building. "What's he talking about?"

"I don't know. He said squirrels took his ax."

"Huh. I'll take Levi out to his place and we'll make sure he can chop his firewood. Or just do it for him again. That might be the problem."

One of the large garage bay doors rumbled open, and we stopped just before reaching the concrete driveway. The engine lights flashed.

"Uh-oh, they must have gotten a call. Do you have to go?"

"No."

The engine pulled out of the station, but it didn't seem to be in any hurry. It stopped, and I realized there was something strung up on the side of it. A banner. It read...

Oh my god.

I gasped, my mouth falling open. The banner on the side of the fire engine read *Grace, will you marry me?* in bright red letters.

"Asher—" I started to speak, but stopped short. He was down on one knee.

Taking my hand, he smiled up at me, and my heart nearly exploded. "Grace, you're my best friend and the love of my life. You're it for me. I want to spend the rest of our lives making you happy. Will you marry me?"

Trembling and nodding, with tears running down my cheeks, I gave him the only answer I ever could. "Yes."

It took me a second to realize he was holding a box. Then slipping a ring on my finger. Everything was a blur of tears and giggles and kisses and *I love you*s. Arms thrown around his neck. My feet lifting off the ground.

He put me down and I took a deep breath, trying to

collect myself. I looked down at my shaking hand, at the ring shining on my finger.

"Do you like it?" He tucked my hair behind my ear.

"I love it so much. I love you so much. Oh my god, we're getting married."

He smiled again, his dimples puckering in his cheeks. "We sure are. I love you, Grace."

It was about then that I realized applause was coming from the garage bay. Chief Stanley and a bunch of the crew walked out, clapping, whooping, and hollering. Logan cupped his hands around his mouth to shout his congratulations and Levi smiled at us as he clapped.

But it wasn't just the fire department. Gavin and Gram were there, and so were my mom and Elijah. A crowd of our friends and neighbors emerged, clapping and smiling. Someone had balloons and people started setting up tables on the grass. A couple of the firefighters hung a big *Congratulations Asher and Grace* banner on the side of the building. It looked like half the town was here.

"Oh my god. You did all this?"

"Yeah. Originally it was just going to be the banner, but you know how people are around here. It turned into a surprise engagement party pretty quickly."

"I guess it's a good thing I said yes." I nudged him.

He slid his arms around me. "I never had any doubt."

Neither did I. I think a part of me had always known I'd marry Asher Bailey. And I'd been right.

13

GRACE

The bar was so crowded, we were lucky to have gotten a pool table. I chalked the end of my cue, as if that was going to help my game. At least I wasn't playing against Asher. He sat off to the side with a beer in his hand and a little smile on his face, watching me. I'd been making sure to bend over in front of him as often as possible. Which wasn't helping my game, but it was fun.

We had come out with a few guys from the fire station and their girlfriends to a bar near the college. It was packed tonight—a mix of locals and college students. Everyone in town knew this place had the best nachos, so it tended to fill up, especially on a Saturday night. The din of voices was so loud it drowned out the music playing in the background.

Tamara took a shot and missed. Fortunately for me, my opponents were about as good as I was—which wasn't saying much. The guys had graciously insisted the girls play first, which really meant they wanted to do what Asher was doing—sit back and watch us bend over the table.

I took a drink of my beer, then set it down. Leaning over

the table, I lined up a shot and took it. The ball rolled right into the corner pocket.

"Yes!" I pumped my fist into the air and tossed a look over my shoulder at Asher. "Did you see that?"

"I saw it. Nice one, beautiful."

"Thanks."

I glanced into the crowd near the bar and accidentally locked eyes with Josiah Haven. He was tall and thickly built, his beard and plaid flannel shirt giving him a lumberjack vibe. A common look around here.

Josiah's gaze flicked from me to Asher. They didn't exchange a glare, exactly—it was more like a mutual agreement to ignore each other. This bar was close enough to the college to be neutral territory. I didn't really know Josiah, but I got the impression that he had no more interest in starting trouble than Asher did. His eyes flicked over me, then he walked away, disappearing into the crowd.

Asher tipped his beer bottle to see how much was left, then gestured to mine. "Want another one?"

I wasn't quite finished, but it was only my first. "Sure, I'll take another."

He got up and gave me a quick kiss. "I'll be right back."

The other guys—Matt, Randy, and Christian—left with Asher to get more drinks. The bar was packed; it would be a while before they got back.

Alex, Randy's girlfriend, played her turn. Then Jess was up. I liked them, although I'd only hung out with them as a group of couples, never just the girls. Still, we had a nice time when we went out. I missed my friends from college, but I was gradually rebuilding my social life here.

I certainly had no regrets about my decision to stay.

Tamara put her cue back on the stand. "I need to go to the ladies' room."

"Me too," Alex said, and Jess grabbed her purse.

"You coming, Grace?" Tamara asked.

I glanced at the table. We'd probably lose it if we all left. "That's okay, I'll hold our place here."

"You sure?" Jess asked.

"Yeah, I don't mind."

The girls left down the little hallway toward the restrooms. I had to admit, it was true what they said about girls going to the bathroom in groups.

Asher and the guys were still waiting at the bar, so I decided to take a few practice shots. I knew the girls wouldn't mind—none of us were serious enough about the game to care about the score. I wandered around to the other side of the table and picked a potential shot. Leaned over and lined up my cue.

I felt someone behind me, his body skimming my ass, and I wondered how Asher had gotten back so fast. "Watch it, big guy, I'm playing here."

Hands rested on my hips and he pressed his groin against me. My heart rate jumped. That wasn't Asher.

Straightening quickly, I whipped around, and my cue clattered to the floor. I had the fleeting thought that I should have held onto it in case I needed to hit this guy with it, but it was too late for that. My hands landed on his chest and I pushed.

"Get the fuck off me."

He staggered back a step, his eyebrows lifting in surprise. I didn't recognize him. Short blond hair, square jaw. The Tilikum College t-shirt probably meant he was a student.

"Whoa, hey." He put his hands up.

"What the hell? You don't just walk up to some girl and grab her ass like that."

"When she's wearing shorts like those, you do." His eyes swept up and down. "Damn, girl."

I couldn't tell if he was drunk, or just that much of an asshole. Maybe both. He had a bunch of buddies behind him, most of them holding beers. A few of them elbowed each other, snickering.

"If that was supposed to be a pickup line, it sucked."

His friends moved, fanning out around the pool table. They acted casual, but I didn't like the way they made me feel penned in. I glanced toward the bar, but I couldn't see Asher from where I was standing.

"Okay, you're right. I'm sorry, princess." He took a step closer. "Give me another chance."

"I'm not your princess. And I'm engaged, so you're wasting your time."

"Oh shit, is he here?" the guy asked. "Hey, you guys, wanna watch me take some dude's fiancée out from under him?"

One of his friends sat on the edge of the table. "Yeah, right."

"You don't think I can do it?"

Warnings were going off in my head like a fire alarm. I needed to get away. The guy had me backed up against the pool table, so I tried to move past him, shoving him aside with my arm.

His hand clamped around my wrist. I twisted, shouting for him to let go, and an instant later chaos erupted around me.

I stumbled a few steps before regaining my feet and whipping around. A knot of men had formed next to the pool table—shoving each other, voices raised. Asher was in the middle of it.

An arm hooked around my waist and pulled me back,

whoever it was telling me to get clear. Matt, Randy, and Christian were in the thick of the fray with Asher. The group seemed to swell, people pouring in around the pool tables. I couldn't tell what was happening, or if the asshole who'd grabbed me was even still in there. Someone moved in front of me, pointing their phone, ready to record.

"Asher, don't," I shouted, but I had no idea if he could hear me. I certainly couldn't see anything.

It looked like shoving broke out in the middle. More yelling. My stomach knotted. I kept getting pushed further back by the crowd.

Someone grabbed my arm. It was Tamara.

"What's going on?"

"I don't know. Some dicks were harassing me." I got up on my tiptoes, trying to see. "The guys came back, but I can't tell what's happening in there."

"I think the bar staff is breaking it up," she said. "I just saw the bouncer muscle his way in."

That was a relief. Tamara and I pushed through the crowd to get closer. It didn't seem like things were calming down, but it didn't sound like anyone was throwing punches, either.

Except... oh no.

I stepped around a guy in a baseball cap in time to see Asher taking slow steps backward, his hands up as if to indicate he wasn't a threat. Matt, Christian, and Randy were with him, and the bouncers were herding all four of them toward the front.

Great. They were getting kicked out of the bar.

Why the fuck were *they* getting kicked out? Where was the asshole who'd been harassing me?

At least some of his dickhead buddies were getting

kicked out too. Another bouncer was ushering several of them out the door.

"Asher," I called, although I knew he wouldn't hear me over all the noise. I waved and he met my eyes, his expression apologetic. I mouthed that I'd be right there.

"Do you think they're going to get in trouble?" Tamara asked.

"I don't know, but we better get out there. I just need to get my purse."

"Okay," Tamara said. "We'll meet you out front."

God, what a mess.

The crowd inside was already dispersing now that the show was over, although a group still bunched around the pool table. I didn't see my purse where I'd left it, but maybe it had gotten knocked over in the commotion. I circled around, back toward the restrooms. More yelling broke out near the front door. One of the asshole's buddies was shouting at the bouncer.

Dumbass.

An arm grabbed me from behind and a hand clamped over my mouth before I could so much as gasp. I tried to break free, but my feet dragged across the floor and a second later I was in the dark hallway outside the men's room. Another set of arms grabbed my legs, hoisting them up.

What the fuck was happening? And how could they be so strong?

I thrashed as hard as I could, but there was nothing I could do against the force of all that muscle, bone, and sinew. They hauled me through a door and cool night air hit my face. My heart raced and I could feel the flood of panic trying to take hold. Where were they taking me?

Someone grunted. Another guy laughed, a harsh snicker that sent a sharp stab of fear down my spine.

"Get her down."

It was all happening so fast. Rough hands shoved me to the ground. A weight slammed over my hips—someone straddling me. I managed a strangled yell before the hand gripped my face harder, making it hard to breathe.

"Hold her."

Someone jerked my arms over my head and the weight on top of me made it impossible to move. Tears leaked out of the corners of my eyes. Tears of fear and rage.

A face moved down, close to mine. It was him. "Hey, princess. Told you I was going to take you."

I tried to struggle, but his weight held me down.

"Go ahead, princess." His breath smelled like beer. "I like it when they fight back. Makes me hard."

Someone laughed. I couldn't see how many guys were here, but he had help.

"I go second."

"You'll wait your fucking turn," the guy on top of me said.

"Come on, fucking do it. There's people right out there."

Oh god. No. Please, no.

I thrashed harder, but I could barely move. Blood pounded in my ears and my vision blurred.

Footsteps. Were those footsteps? Shouting started again. Male voices yelling. Swearing. A woman's shriek. The weight on top of me lifted and air rushed into my lungs. I scrambled to my feet, gasping for breath, and there were hands, then arms around me. Ushering me toward a street-light. Friendly arms. Women's arms. My eyes still blurred with tears, fear and anger making me shake.

"What's happening?"

I spun around. Alex and Jess had me. They'd pulled me out to the street, around the corner in front of the bar. I couldn't see into the alley.

Matt and Christian shoved two of the asshole's buddies away from the bar, near the entrance to the alley. They were shouting. Pushing. Randy had another one up against the wall.

Where was Asher?

"No." I lurched for the alley, but Alex and Jess held me back.

Red and blue lights flashed behind me, the light reflecting off the bar's darkened windows. My stomach turned over and I was afraid I'd throw up.

My ears felt muffled, like I'd been plunged underwater. Cops ran past, into the alley. Alex was trying to talk to me—ask me what happened and if I was okay. Or maybe it was Jess. I didn't know.

For a long, sickening moment, it seemed as if everything was caught in stasis. No one moving. Just the red and blue lights, blinding in the night.

"Miss? Miss?"

Someone was trying to get my attention, but all I could do was stare in horror as a figure emerged from the alley. Asher. His arms were behind his back, his wrists secured in handcuffs.

Handcuffs.

"Asher!"

His jaw was clenched tight, his eyes on the ground. Was that blood on his shirt? Was he hurt? The cops led him out to the street, one on each side, holding him by the elbows.

"Miss?"

"What?" I asked, barely registering that a deputy was

trying to talk to me. A siren rang out and more lights flashed. I was dimly aware of paramedics. More cops.

"No! Asher!"

All I could do was stare. He looked over his shoulder, and for the space of a heartbeat, he met my gaze. His eyes were wild and afraid, like a bear being shoved into a cage.

They put him in the backseat. Shut the door. And drove away.

14
———

ASHER

I should have felt something. My knuckles were battered and raw. When I flexed my hands, a part of my brain registered the pain. But I didn't really feel it. It was like I'd been dosed with anesthesia, only I was awake and able to move. It wasn't natural.

The gnawing ache in my chest and the heavy knot of dread in my gut were another story. Those were acute and painful—and unavoidable. Like the image of Grace on the ground, pinned down in that alley, surrounded. Asleep or awake, it haunted me. As did the truth of what I'd done.

A guy was fucking dead because of me.

The last seventy-two hours had been a never-ending nightmare. The kind that leaves you gasping for breath and grabbing your chest until you're flooded with relief because you realize you were dreaming.

Except there was no relief. I wasn't asleep. The nightmare was real.

And every day it got worse.

I sat in an interview room in the sheriff's office with my defense attorney, Sean Nelson. He was young, wearing a suit. He carried a leather briefcase that matched the color of his shoes and I had no idea why I noticed that.

The room felt hollow, like there wasn't enough air. It was hard to breathe.

It had been less than seventy-two hours since my arrest, and I'd already been in front of the judge twice. I'd listened while he denied bail, citing my previous record—the assault charge when I was seventeen.

And I'd stood in court this morning to receive the formal charges. Second-degree murder.

I was fucked.

"I know today probably seemed like bad news," Sean said. "And I'll be honest, I'm a little surprised the prosecutor decided to be a hardass and charge you with murder, rather than manslaughter."

I nodded to show I was listening, but my eyes were locked on the table.

"We knew they'd factor in your prior assault charge and bring up your martial arts training, so that wasn't a surprise. But don't panic. The state will often start with a more serious charge to leave some room to negotiate it down with a plea bargain."

"Negotiate it down to what?"

"If they won't drop the charges entirely, I'm going to push for manslaughter in the second degree. The sentencing for first-degree manslaughter is harsher, but both are better than murder. Obviously I can't promise anything, but given the circumstances, and the state of mind you were in, I don't think you're ultimately going to face murder charges for this."

I nodded again, but clenched my fists as rage spread through my gut. I could still see it. Feel it. That sickening moment when I'd realized they had her.

He shuffled some paperwork. "Now, the vast majority of cases don't go to trial, but I'll know more when I meet with the prosecutor."

"If it went to trial, it would be for murder?"

"Yes. Considering that your actions were in the defense of your fiancée, and that we have witnesses who can testify to what the victim and his friends were about to do to her, we'd have a case. But unless the prosecutor won't budge on the murder charge, I'm going to highly recommend we take the plea deal."

I scrubbed my hands through my hair. A plea bargain would mean accepting whatever my attorney could negotiate with the prosecutor. A couple of people in business suits with law degrees were supposed to decide my future?

But I didn't want to subject my family—Gram, my brothers, Grace—to a trial. And what were the chances a trial would go in my favor? Would a jury let me walk after what I'd done?

I had a feeling I knew the answer to that.

"Let's assume we reach a plea agreement," he continued. "What happens after that is a plea hearing. It's not a full-blown trial, but it's more involved than the arraignment today. The judge hears the charges and sentencing recommendations that we've agreed to. And both sides have an opportunity to make statements. Ultimately, sentencing is up to the judge, but they usually go by the recommendation in the agreement."

"And then?"

He paused. "Even if we get the charges reduced, it will still mean prison time."

"When would I go?"

"To prison?"

I nodded.

"You'd be transferred into the custody of the state at the end of the plea hearing. From there, you'd be transported directly to the prison facility."

I let that sink in for a moment. "People can attend the hearing?"

"Yes, it's a public proceeding."

They were going to be there. Grace was going to be there.

Fuck.

She'd come with Gram and my brothers to the arraignment today. It had been fucking torture, knowing she was so close. Knowing she was hurting and there was nothing I could do for her. I couldn't hold her, kiss her, touch her. I couldn't fix this.

Everything was fucked to hell. And there was nothing I could do. I'd never felt so out of control.

"Hang in there, Asher," he said. "I'm going to do everything I can."

Deputy Spangler came in to escort me back to my cell. Gave me a sympathetic look. He'd been a senior when I was a freshman, and I'd been at his wedding last year.

One night, and everything was different.

He led me to the cell block. I was the only one back here. The first night, they'd been holding another guy, but he was gone now. I went in and Deputy Spangler shut the bars behind me.

"She tried to come see you, by the way," he said. "Grace did. We wanted to let her, but we couldn't. It's policy. But now that the arraignment's over, I think we'll be able to allow a visitor."

"Thanks." I sank down onto the edge of the narrow bed.

"Your brothers came down here too."

"Oh shit, what'd they do?"

He shook his head. "Nothing. Just asked to see you."

I let out a relieved breath. The last thing we needed was my brothers doing something stupid.

"What about the Havens?" I asked. "They must be all over this."

"Not really. Far as I know, they've been quiet about it."

That was good. If any of them tried to use this as an excuse to fuck with my family—

What would I do? Nothing. I was locked in a cage. The world could be burning down, and there'd be nothing I could do about it.

"We've been getting a ton of phone calls, though. Whole town's in an uproar."

I could only imagine. No doubt my great aunt Tillie had already called the mayor—she loved to remind people she'd given him piano lessons—and my cousin Chuck, Tilikum's resident conspiracy theorist, was probably busy creating a *Free Asher* campaign.

Not that it would do any good. Hell, my entire family could camp out around the courthouse and it wouldn't make a difference. It wasn't like they could change the justice system.

And they couldn't change what I'd done.

Neither could I. I couldn't go back in time. Couldn't take it back.

And the really fucked-up thing? I didn't know if I would.

15

GRACE

I'd never been so exhausted in my entire life. It was only mid-afternoon, but I lay on Gram's couch, feeling like a wrung-out washrag—dingy and tattered. I hadn't slept much since Asher's arrest, and none of it in my own bed. I'd been staying here since Saturday night.

My mom had brought me clean clothes before the arraignment this morning. She seemed to understand without me explaining that I had to be here, with his family. She hadn't told Elijah yet, but he knew something was wrong.

Except it wasn't just something. *Everything* was wrong.

The words ran through my mind over and over. *Murder in the second degree.*

Gavin sat on the floor near my feet with his back against the couch. His face was buried in his hoodie while he played a game on his phone. It was like the boys were taking shifts; at least one of them was always with me. Levi had started it, sleeping on the floor next to me the first night. Logan had taken over Sunday morning, lingering nearby—talking if I wanted to, remaining silent if I didn't. They hadn't left me alone since.

I was so grateful.

Shifting on the couch, I tried to get comfortable. My back was bruised from the assault, making me wince every time I turned over. Still, I'd been lucky. It could have been so much worse. A part of me knew that at some point, I'd have to deal with what had happened to me. But right now, I didn't care about any of that.

All I cared about was Asher.

Gavin leaned his head back on the couch cushion and turned his face toward me. "Need anything?"

"Not right now. But thanks."

He nodded and went back to his phone.

Knowing how grateful I felt to not be alone made me hurt for Asher even more. Because he wasn't just alone, he was in jail. The stupid judge had denied bail. Everyone had seemed surprised by that, and I still didn't understand why. Because he'd gotten in a fight in high school? Someone had mentioned the concern that Asher would try to retaliate against the guy's friends. The ones who'd been involved were facing charges, but they'd all been released from jail for the time being.

Could the judge really think Asher was the kind of man who'd hurt someone—or worse—in cold blood? God, I hoped not. If he did, we didn't have much hope he'd be lenient.

Evan came downstairs and settled into an armchair next to the couch. His beard was getting thick. He'd come home Sunday, dropping everything on a moment's notice to be here for his family.

Of course he had. He was a Bailey. That was what they did.

The fridge and freezer were stuffed with food, dropped off by a steady stream of family members and neighbors. They were rallying around Asher's family, offering what support they could. We'd had offers to picket the sheriff's office or the courthouse, promises to organize a letter-writing campaign, and heartfelt assurances of calling in favors to make sure Asher went free.

I appreciated the gestures, but I knew ultimately none of it would help.

Levi and Logan wandered into the living room. Trying not to wince, I sat up to make room. Logan wedged himself between me and the couch's arm, even though there wasn't really enough space. I gratefully leaned against him. Levi was more subtle in his support, sitting in the other corner but giving my foot a gentle squeeze.

"Is Gram still out?" Levi asked.

Gram had declared that she was going to the store because she needed to do something normal. Then she'd dared her grandsons to stop her. They'd wisely let her go.

I nodded. "Yeah."

"Look, I know none of us want to talk about this, but we need to," Logan said. "Is he going to go to prison?"

My stomach went queasy at the mention of prison.

We all looked at each other, full of fear and worry. Because we didn't know what was going to happen. We'd all been at the arraignment. We'd heard the charges.

It felt like we were on a runaway train with no brakes. Out of control, hurtling toward the end of the line where the tracks were unfinished. To a chasm with no bridge.

"How could they charge him with murder?" Gavin asked.

"Right? That piece of shit was going to..." Logan trailed off, like he didn't want to finish the sentence in front of me.

"Any man would have done what Asher did. He was saving Grace, not trying to kill anyone."

"It doesn't help that he knows how," Evan said quietly.

"Knows how to what?" Logan asked.

"Kill someone."

"Fuck that. So he took jiujitsu. Why the hell does that matter?"

"He's right," Levi said. "In court it matters. So does his assault charge."

I tucked my hair behind my ear. "The lawyer said the state will probably accept a plea bargain with reduced charges. That means he won't go to trial for murder."

The lawyer had seemed confident when he'd met with us briefly after the arraignment. He'd assured us today's court appearance was just one step in the process. Told us not to panic.

That was easier said than done. Especially after I'd looked up the sentencing guidelines for manslaughter. Murder in the second degree was worse, of course. That could mean as much as life in prison. But manslaughter meant prison, too.

"There isn't much we can do, except wait." Evan turned his gaze directly on Logan. "And stay out of trouble."

"Why are you looking at me?"

"I'm just saying the last thing we need is another Bailey behind bars. Don't do anything stupid."

Logan grumbled something incoherent and slumped back against the couch.

I leaned my head against Logan's shoulder and twisted my ring around my finger. I wished I could at least see him. I'd tried on Sunday morning, but they'd told me no visitors. It hadn't helped much that they'd been apologetic about it.

I'd wanted to yell at them. To lose my cool and scream

that it wasn't fair. Instead, I'd accepted their assurances that I'd be able to see him soon, and left.

Left him there. Alone.

My breath felt shaky and tears stung my eyes. I chewed on the inside of my lip, fighting them back. I couldn't fall apart. Not now. I had to stay strong.

I didn't know what tomorrow was going to bring. My future was once again hazy, the road I traveled shrouded in fog. But I knew one thing: I wasn't giving up on him. Not now. Not ever.

No matter what happened, no matter how bad things got, Asher was mine. And I would always belong to him.

16

ASHER

y heart thumped uncomfortably hard and I shook my leg under the table. Sitting still was impossible. I was too agitated. There was nothing like robbing a man of all semblance of control over his life to make him restless.

Sean took the seat across from me. He'd met with the prosecutor this morning, but I couldn't tell anything by his expression.

"Here's where we are," he began, his tone all business. "The prosecution agreed to reduce the charges, so it's no longer murder. It's manslaughter. Unfortunately, they're insisting on manslaughter in the first degree, instead of second."

"What does that mean?"

"It means a longer sentence. The standard range is six and a half to eight and a half years for someone without a criminal history. The prosecutor agreed to eight. That's a win, considering you have a prior assault charge."

Eight years. I shifted in my seat.

"I highly recommend you take this. If it goes to trial,

you're back to facing second-degree murder charges. Yes, you were defending your fiancée, and most people would understand that. But Asher, the eye-witness accounts support the prosecution's assertion that your martial arts training means you have to be held to a different standard. The police reports show you tore through two men to get to the victim. That took more than blind rage, it took skill. They'll argue that you should have stopped when you neutralized the threat—before the altercation turned deadly."

My chest felt like it was being crushed. Deep down, I knew he was right. As much as I wanted to fight my way out of this, I couldn't. There wasn't a way out.

"Do you need some time to think about it?" he asked.

"No." My voice ground out of my throat. "I'll accept it."

He nodded slowly, and I didn't miss the sympathy in his expression. "You're making the right decision, Asher. I'll notify the prosecutor. You'll remain here until the plea hearing."

"When will that be?"

"Probably a week."

"That fast?"

"Yeah. In a small community like this, the courts aren't usually too backlogged. Things move quickly, especially with a plea bargain."

I rubbed the back of my neck, still shaking my leg. Fuck, this was really happening.

"Is there anything else I can do for you?"

"Can I see anyone?"

"I should be able to arrange for a visitor. Do you want to see Grace?"

Just hearing her name felt like a knife to the chest. It

took me a second to reply, and when I did, my voice was hoarse. "Yeah. Please."

"Okay."

ANOTHER DAY WENT by before I heard anything. It gave me time to let it all sink in. In some ways, I felt better. The uncertainty had been driving me crazy. At least now I knew.

I tried to cling to the fact that it wasn't life in prison. It was eight years. I'd be getting out by the time I was thirty.

But eight years in a state penitentiary was a long fucking time.

And when it was over, it wasn't like I'd be able to come home and pick up where I'd left off, as if it had been nothing but an interruption. I'd be a convicted felon. Unlike my juvenile assault charge, it couldn't be sealed someday. It was never going away. I'd always have a record.

Which meant I'd never be a career firefighter. Never be a fire inspector, or one day fire chief. All my plans for my life, everything I'd been working toward—it was all gone.

And now I had a mountain to climb. One that was brutal and mercilessly cold. There was only one thing I could do. Survive. And it was going to take everything I had.

Like a man planning for his impending death, I wrote letters to Gram and my brothers. I let them know how sorry I was to have done this to them. How much I hated that I had to leave them like this. I told Gram I loved her, and not to worry about me. To focus on my brothers, because they'd need her more than ever. And I told my brothers to keep their shit together, and to take care of each other, no matter what.

But Grace... I had to face her in person. I knew what I

had to do. It was going to rip my insides out to do it, but I didn't have any other choice. I had to do what was best for both of us. For her, because she deserved a future. And for me, because this was the only way I'd survive.

THE HANDCUFFS BIT into my wrists. I twisted my hands, feeling the pull of cold metal. Deputy Spangler had apologized for having to cuff me before taking me to the interview room. I told him I understood.

I felt strangely calm. Almost numb again. Somewhere in the back of my brain, I knew I was doing it on purpose. Pulling away. Constructing defenses. I was coming to terms with my fate—with my future. I hated it, but it was inevitable.

The door opened and I almost couldn't look up. Grace paused and her eyes landed on me, her heartbreak written all over her face.

And something inside me broke.

This was my fucking fault. I wasn't going to make this worse. I'd ruined my life. I sure as hell wasn't going to keep ruining hers.

Deputy Spangler directed her to the other chair. She didn't have anything with her. No purse. Not even a coat. They must have searched her before letting her come back here.

At least I wasn't behind a glass wall. That was one good thing about this small-town sheriff's office.

Spangler gave me a short nod, then left the room, closing the door behind him. I had no idea if he was supposed to leave us alone or not, but I was grateful to not have an audience.

"Hey." Grace's voice shook. "I want to ask if you're okay, but of course you're not."

"How are you?"

"I don't know. Okay, but also terrible."

I nodded. "They told me you weren't injured."

"No, just a little bruising, but it's not bad."

A wave of emotion crashed over me. My chest felt like I was trapped under a pile of bricks, the weight crushing my lungs.

"Asher, I—"

"I'm accepting the plea bargain," I said, interrupting her. I needed to get this out. "First-degree manslaughter. Eight years in prison."

Her lips parted, and for a second, she didn't speak. "So... that's it?"

"That's it. No trial."

"You mean, it's official? It's done?"

"There's going to be another hearing. After that it's over."

"Can you change your mind? Can you tell them—"

"No. This is my best option."

Tears filled her eyes and I forced myself to maintain eye contact. To not look away. "But... eight years?"

I nodded. "Yeah."

Swiping beneath her eyes, she took a deep breath. Straightened in her chair. "Okay. Eight years. It could have been worse, right? This is fine. We can do this."

I put my hands on the table so she could see the hand-cuffs. "No, Grace. *We* are not doing this."

"What?"

"*I* have to do this. This burden is on me, not you."

She shifted away slightly, eying me with suspicion. "What do you mean?"

I took a deep breath, steeling myself for what I was about to say. What I had to say. "None of this is your fault. And I'm so fucking sorry, Grace. But it's over. You're not going to wait for me, and we're not getting married when I get out."

"Excuse me?"

"I don't want this any more than you do. I don't want any of it. But I have to live through it. I don't have a choice. And I refuse—I fucking refuse—to ruin your life any more than I already have."

"You haven't—"

"Listen to me. Please." My voice broke and I swallowed down the emotion threatening to choke me. "You have to take that ring off and move on. Go back to school. To WSU —don't stay here in this town. Finish your degree and then start your life. I can't give you a future. Not anymore. You have to go out there and live your life. Find someone who makes you happy. It's what you deserve."

She stared at me with her mouth slightly open, as if she couldn't believe what she was hearing.

"Grace, you have to let me go."

I needed to cut this short. Letting her go was the hardest thing I was ever going to do, and if I stayed with her much longer, I'd crack. I couldn't afford that. If I walked through those prison gates wounded and bleeding, they'd rip me to shreds.

I had to be hard. Impenetrable.

"Spangler?"

"Asher, don't."

The deputy opened the door and poked his head in.

I stood.

"Asher."

Spangler's eyes flicked between me and Grace. I jerked

my head in the direction of the holding cells, and he nodded.

I stepped out ahead of him.

"Asher, don't do this."

He fell in step behind me. I didn't ignore Grace's pleas for me to wait. I heard them. Let them sink in. They were a conviction and punishment all their own. The price I had to pay for what I'd done.

17

GRACE

The courtroom was packed. Only a handful of people had been here for the arraignment, but today it seemed like half the town was stuffed into the bench seats. The air was thick and stuffy, the temperature uncomfortably warm.

Gram sat next to me, holding my hand firmly in hers. Levi sat on her right, holding her other hand. She was seventy years old, sitting in a courtroom waiting to hear the fate of her oldest grandson. You'd think her hands would have been clasped with ours to give her strength. But she was the one supporting us. Her strength giving us hope.

The rest of Asher's brothers were in a line on my left. Logan couldn't seem to sit still. His leg shook next to mine, but I didn't tell him to stop.

As for Asher, he hadn't looked back. Not even once.

I'd told everyone about the plea bargain, so they knew what was coming. We also knew there was a chance the judge would impose a different sentence than the recommendation in the plea deal. It could be longer. This could all be about to get worse.

Or maybe the judge would go easy on him. Perhaps six years instead of eight? Maybe five?

I'd been silently praying, pleading, hoping for a shorter sentence. Willing the judge to show some mercy. To give Asher a break.

I hadn't told his family everything else Asher had said.

To take off my ring.

Go back to school.

Find someone else to make me happy.

Move on.

Let him go.

He'd broken up with me.

In the moments after he'd been led away by Deputy Spangler, I'd been numb with shock. I'd left the sheriff's office in a daze, my heart in my throat.

Instead of going straight home, I'd driven around for a while. Finally I found myself stopped outside the old house on Evergreen Street.

It was about then that I'd gotten mad.

I'd flown out of my car, seething with anger, and started throwing things. Rocks, sticks, pinecones, anything I could find. I'd yelled, and cried, and hurled things at the side of the house.

Fortunately, I hadn't broken any windows.

I was still mad. Furious, in fact. I was hurt and angry and frustrated. I'd been assaulted, and that one vile act had been like a bomb going off, ripping my life to shreds. I didn't want anyone to be dead, but this entire thing was his fault. If he hadn't dragged me out of that bar, none of this would have happened. He'd still be alive, and Asher wouldn't be facing criminal charges and prison time.

We'd be planning a wedding. Not sitting in court,

waiting for a judge to tell us how bad the future was going to be.

I shifted on the hard bench, but there was no getting comfortable. Gram squeezed my hand and I squeezed back.

We'd listened to the details of the plea agreement. The charges and suggested sentencing. Sat through the prosecution's statement, followed by the defense. There had been explanations of the law and how it had been applied. The prosecution had given the reasons Asher deserved to be incarcerated. The defense had outlined the arguments for leniency in sentencing.

And now it was time for Asher to speak.

The judge called on him to stand. He got to his feet, still not casting a single glance behind him.

"Mr. Bailey, do you understand the charges brought forth against you?"

"Yes."

"And are you making an intelligent and knowing waiver of your rights and making this plea of your own free will?"

"I am."

"Mr. Bailey has entered a plea of guilty to the charge of manslaughter in the first degree, as agreed upon by the state. The court has taken the sentencing recommendation into account. Asher Bailey, this court sentences you to eight years in a state penitentiary."

The judge continued speaking, but the details of his words were lost to me. Eight years. They were taking him away from me for eight years.

Worse, he had to survive in prison for eight fucking years.

By the time I realized I was crying, my cheeks were already wet with tears. Gram still held my hand, her grip sure and steady. Logan had thrown an arm around my shoulder, hugging me tight.

Oh god. He was going to prison.

A man in uniform approached Asher. He held his hands in front of him while the man handcuffed him.

And then he was being led away.

"Wait, they're taking him now?" Logan asked. "We don't even get to see him first?"

"No," I said, my voice flat. I'd asked the attorney what would happen, so I already knew. They'd transport him to the prison today. "They're taking him now."

He seemed to move in slow motion. Hands in front, bound by metal. Head down. Every step he took opened the wound in my heart a little more, threatening to rip it in two. Vaguely, I wondered if I'd bleed to death.

Without looking back, Asher followed the man in uniform through a door. And just like that, he was gone.

18

DEAR ASHER

ear Asher,

I'M STILL NOT sure how to begin this letter. I think I've started it a dozen times. You should see the pile of crumpled paper in the garbage can next to my desk. It's ridiculous. But nothing seems right. What am I supposed to do, ask you how you've been?

I'll just get straight to the point.

Fuck you, Asher.

I'm sorry to pick a fight with you right now, of all times. But you are not breaking up with me.

I understand why you said the things you did. I realize you're trying to do what you think is best for me, and I appreciate that. I really do.

But no, I will not take off your ring. No, I will not find someone else. No, I will not move on. No, I will not let you go.

That's not how this works.

You are what's best for me. I love you, and I've loved you for most of my life. That hasn't changed, and it isn't going to.

This is not the end of our life together. This is a great big, soul-sucking, heart-wrenching tragedy. But it will only ruin us if we let it. And I refuse to let that happen.

Your only job right now is to survive. Don't let them break you. Do what you have to do to get through each day. I'm counting on you to make it through to the end.

I'll be out here, doing the same thing.

And let me be perfectly clear about this, Asher Bailey. I'm not going anywhere. Eight years is an interruption, not a lifetime. We can survive this. I realize nothing will ever be the same. You'll be different, and so will I.

But when you walk out those prison doors, you'll come home to me. I'll be waiting for you, with your ring still on my finger.

LOVE ALWAYS,

Grace

BONUS EPILOGUE
GRACE

Note: This bonus epilogue also appears at the end of Gaining Miles: The Miles Family Book Five. It takes place six years after this book, Protecting You, and two years after the end of the Miles Family series.

I stood outside the house, a set of keys dangling from my fingers. *My* keys. A jolt of excitement sent a little shiver down my spine. I'd done it. I'd planned and saved for years for this. And today, after signing paperwork until my hand felt like it was going to fall off, the house was mine.

A tangle of blackberry bushes covered the front window —most of the windows, actually. The front yard was knee-high grass and weeds, the fence was rotting, and that was just the outside. The interior was going to be a total gut job. At least the structure was sound. It needed a lot of drywall repair, but the walls were sturdy, and the roof was good.

The rest? It was pretty much a disaster. It needed a new

kitchen, new bathrooms, new flooring, new paint, new windows. My realtor had tried to talk me out of buying it. As had my mom.

But this was more than just a house. It was a dream. A dream I was fighting to keep alive.

Asher and I had walked by this house on the way home from school every day for years. Most kids crossed to the other side of the street, calling it haunted or creepy. Not me and Asher. We'd both loved the old abandoned house on Evergreen Street. Years ago, we'd made a pact that we'd buy this house, together. It was where we were going to live our life. Start our family.

The plan had been to buy it after we were married. But those plans had been interrupted. Asher wasn't here. He was in prison.

Another shiver ran down my spine, but this one wasn't excitement. It was cold fear. It ran through my veins whenever I thought about Asher and what he was going through.

I took a deep breath. Smelled the fresh air and shook off my dark thoughts. There wasn't anything I could do about Asher right now. He wouldn't be gone forever. And when he got out, he'd come back to a dream that I'd turned into reality. Our dream. This house.

A strange way to cope with your fiancé being in prison? Probably. But I wasn't going to sit around doing nothing for eight years while I waited for him to come home.

My phone rang and I pulled it out of my pocket. It was Shannon, my father's ex-wife. My mother had unknowingly been the other woman in an affair, having two children with Lawrence Miles—me and my much younger brother, Elijah. Four years ago, I'd gone looking for my father—he'd gone deadbeat dad on my little brother—and discovered he was not only married, but had four other children.

It had been a shock to everyone, but my new family had embraced me and Elijah—and my mom. Mom had become good friends with Shannon. We'd been at Shannon's wedding two years ago when she'd married Ben Gaines. And when my mom had married Jack Cordero last year, Shannon had been her matron of honor.

I swiped to answer her call. "Hey, Shannon. Aren't you still in Barbados?"

"We are," Shannon said. "But I wanted to call and see if the house closed today."

"It sure did." I walked up to the front door. "I'm here now. I just got the keys."

"Congratulations. Benjamin says congratulations, too."

"Thanks. It's so sweet of you to call."

"Of course," she said. "Send me some pictures if you get the chance. We're here another week, but when we get back, I want to come see it in person."

"Definitely," I said. "Are you guys having fun?"

"This place is paradise," she said, her voice a little dreamy. "We're having a great time."

"I love that. You guys go get a yummy tropical drink or something. Enjoy yourselves. You certainly deserve it."

"Thanks, Grace," she said. "We'll see you next week."

"Bye."

I ended the call and slipped my phone in my back pocket. It was the moment of truth.

The key stuck in the lock. I had to jiggle it to get the doorknob to turn. That was fine, I'd change the locks anyway. That was the first thing Jack had said—*make sure you change the locks, Grace*. I liked my new stepdad. Navigating the new relationship had been a little tricky for me, but he sure did love my mom.

After jiggling the key a little more, I finally got the door open.

The interior was just as dilapidated as I remembered. But all I could see was potential. New paint, new floors, cozy furniture. I was going to take this old abandoned house and turn it into a home.

Before I'd even shut the door, a truck pulled up on the street. I'd invited my siblings to come see the house. My brother Cooper hopped out and pointed through the windshield at his wife, Amelia. It looked like he was telling her to wait. He went around to the passenger side and helped her out, keeping a firm grip on her arm, as if he was afraid she'd fall without him.

Of course, Amelia was a little off-balance. As tall as she was, I was surprised her pregnancy was showing so soon, but she had the cutest baby belly. It hadn't been long after their wedding that they'd announced Amelia was pregnant. I wondered if they knew if the baby was a boy or a girl yet. So far, they hadn't said.

Cooper stopped, his eyes widening as he took in the house. "Holy shit, Gracie, what the hell did you buy? This place is falling apart."

"I told you it was a fixer-upper. Hey, Amelia."

"Hey. The house is..." Amelia glanced around. "I bet it's going to be nice someday, but I kind of agree with Cooper."

I waved a hand. "I know. It's a lot of work, but it'll be fine. The inside is... well, it's not much better, but do you want to see it anyway?"

"Yes," Amelia said brightly. She looked adorable in a light blue t-shirt that said *Beauty and the Bump*.

Cooper had traded his cute husband t-shirts—which had replaced his extensive collection of boyfriend t-shirts—for new dad shirts. The last time I'd seen him, his shirt had said *future awesome daddy*. This one said *Sorry Ladies, This DILF is Taken.*

"Come on in." I moved aside and held the door open.

"You're right, the inside isn't better," Cooper said. He kept a firm grip on Amelia's arm as they stepped over a pile of debris. "Careful, baby."

"Yeah, but it's going to be so beautiful when it's done." I heard another car pull up outside. "I'll see who's here, but you guys are free to look around."

Cooper eyed the place warily, as if dangers to his pregnant wife lurked everywhere.

I went outside and waited on the front step while Leo and Hannah unloaded their little family. Their daughter Madeline was about twenty months, and their newest addition, a son named Zachary, had been born five months ago. Madeline had been a surprise, but they'd loved being parents so much, they hadn't waited long to have another baby.

Leo's hair was shorter than it used to be, but he still had a thick beard. He held Zachary up against his shoulder. Madeline slipped one hand in his, the other in her mom's, as they walked up the path.

"I know," I said, holding up a hand. I could see the doubt on their faces. "It needs a lot of work."

"No, it has so much potential," Hannah said. "I love it."

Motherhood looked great on Hannah. Despite the splotch on her shirt that was probably baby spit-up, she looked fantastic. She and Leo had moved into the house they'd built on Salishan property shortly before Zachary had been born.

"You have such a great eye for color, I'm totally going to pick your brain," I said.

"I'd love to help," Hannah said.

"Uncle Cooper?" Madeline asked, looking up at her dad.

"Yeah, sweetheart, I think Uncle Cooper and Auntie Amelia are already here."

"They're inside," I said. "I don't know if there's anything sharp on the floor, so we'll need to be careful with her."

"I've got her," Hannah said, scooping Madeline up and perching her on her hip. "Should we go see Auntie Grace's new house?"

"Yeah," Madeline said, her little pigtails bobbing as she nodded.

"Go on in," I said. "Cooper and Amelia are in there somewhere."

"We can wait until everyone gets here for the official tour," Leo said.

"Sure," I said. As if on cue, two more cars pulled up. "And here they are."

Brynn and Chase got out with their dog, Scout. Brynn held his leash to keep him from running off.

"Scout, chill," Brynn said. "He loves car rides, but I think he loves getting out in a new place even more."

"Scout, sit," Chase said, his voice authoritative. Scout immediately obeyed and Chase scratched his head. "Good boy."

"Hey, you guys," I said. "Thanks for coming. You can bring Scout inside, but be careful. I don't know what he'll find in there."

"We'll keep an eye on him," Brynn said.

Roland and Zoe had pulled up behind Brynn and Chase. Roland got their three-year-old son, Hudson, out of the car. Zoe was pregnant with their second child, a girl this time.

"Hey, Zoe," I said. "How are you feeling?"

She leaned against the car, resting her hand on her belly.

"Not bad, all things considered. Four weeks and we get to meet her."

"How does Hudson feel about having a baby sister?" I asked.

Zoe shrugged. "He says he's excited. But I think he figures this baby will be like his cousin Zachary. He'll come over and then leave when he gets fussy. We'll see how he feels about her when she's in his house all the time and he has to share his parents with her."

Roland came around, holding Hudson's hand. "Huddy, can you say hi?"

"Hi, Auntie Grace," he said.

"Hi, buddy," I said. "Listen, I told Leo and Hannah this too, but I don't know what you'll find on the floors in there, so just be careful. It's... well, it's a mess."

"No problem." Roland picked up Hudson. "Come on, buddy, let's go check out the new house."

I followed everyone inside, then showed them around. They meandered through the house, peeking in bedrooms and wandering through the kitchen and living rooms. It wasn't very big, but the lot had room to add on if we wanted to, down the road. Of course, making it livable was the first step, and it was going to be a while before that happened.

It was fun to see everyone with their growing families. My family dynamic had changed so much in the last several years. First with discovering four new siblings, then with my mom getting married. They were good changes, but it had taken some time to process.

And it was sad not having Asher here to share in it. We should have been married by now. Maybe even starting our own family. I wrote him letters regularly, so of course I'd told him everything. But when he got home, these people would be strangers to him. Moments like this made my chest ache with the pain of missing him.

"Oh, hey, we're all here," Cooper said, as if just realizing that fact. Glancing at Amelia, he grinned. "Should we tell them?"

"Tell us what?" Brynn asked. "Oh my god, did you find out if the baby is a boy or a girl?"

Amelia's face lit up with a grin to match her husband's. "We did."

The room went quiet, as if everyone was holding their breath. I certainly was.

"Okay, first of all, I knew this from the beginning," Cooper said. "I can even tell you where we conceived, that's how soon I knew she was preggers. We were—"

"Stop," Hannah and Zoe said together.

"Coop, know your audience, buddy," Zoe said, gesturing to the two very curious children looking at him with wide eyes.

"Oh, right," Cooper said. "I'm going to have to get used to that, aren't I? Anyway, I'm just saying I totally called it. Didn't I, Cookie?"

"That's actually true," Amelia said. "I didn't even know I was pregnant, and Cooper looked at me one morning and said I looked pregnant, and he wanted the record to show that he thought it was twin boys. And I said that was probably impossible, but you never know. And we found out yesterday he was right."

The room went dead silent. Even among the dust and debris, you could have heard a pin drop.

"Did you just say twins?" Brynn asked.

Amelia beamed. "Yep. Both boys."

"Holy shit," Leo said. "Two baby Coopers?"

Cooper puffed out his chest and put a protective hand

over Amelia's belly. "Is anyone really surprised? Of course I'd make two babies at once."

"This is amazing," Brynn said, rushing over to hug Amelia.

"Aw, you big goofball," Zoe said, hugging Cooper.

"Congrats, you guys," Roland said. "Wow, life is definitely getting interesting."

"Okay, Chase and Brynn," Zoe said. "When is it your turn?"

Brynn and Chase smiled at each other. "We're talking about it," Brynn said. "Soon."

"Do Mom and Ben know it's twins yet?" Roland asked.

"Nah, we'll tell them when they get back," Cooper said.

Madeline tugged on Leo's pant leg. "Daddy, are Grandma and Grandpa coming?"

"No, sweetheart," Leo said. "They're still on vacation. But they'll be back soon."

I glanced around at our broken-down surroundings. This was sweet, but we didn't need to keep standing around in my dilapidated house. "Well, now that you've seen it, we can go get some food or something. It'll be a while before I'm ready to entertain guests. But there are a bunch of good restaurants in town."

"Okay, but can we talk about how scary this house is?" Cooper asked. "Seriously, Gracie, this place looks like it's going to cave in."

Everyone looked around, murmuring in agreement.

"You know, we can help," Chase said.

"Thank you," I said. "I appreciate that, but I didn't ask you guys to come over here to put you to work."

"Yeah, but—"

Chase was interrupted by the sound of a loud engine

outside. A very loud engine, followed by rowdy voices. I sighed. Of course they were here.

"Hang on a second," I said, and went to the front door.

Four men poured in, still talking to each other. Arguing, really. Typical brothers.

"Guys," I said, raising my voice so they'd hear me.

They all stopped, looking around—whether at the house or my family, I wasn't sure.

"So, guys, these are my brothers and sisters and their families. Roland, Zoe, and their son Hudson. Chase and Brynn, and the furry one is Scout. That's Leo and Hannah, and their little ones are Madeline and Zachary. And that's Cooper and Amelia." I paused to take a breath and gestured to the newcomers. "These guys are my fiancé's brothers. Evan, Levi, Logan, and Gavin Bailey."

"We've met," Logan said, and pointed at Brynn. "I was part of the entertainment at her bachelorette party."

"Oh right, the firefighter," Brynn said.

"Dude," Cooper said, pointing at Levi and Logan. "Are you grown-up twins? We're having twins. It's like seeing into the future."

"Identical," Logan said, glancing at his brother. "Sweet, man. Are yours boys?"

"Yep."

Logan grinned. "Awesome."

"Grace, can we talk about this?" Levi asked, looking around, his brow furrowed. "This place is worse on the inside."

"Exactly," Cooper said. "I like him."

"I know, I know." I put my hands up. "It's a fixer-upper. That means it needs a lot of fixing. But I got a full inspection, so I know what I'm dealing with."

"Can I get a copy of that?" Levi asked, wandering farther inside.

"Later," I said.

Logan put his hands on his hips. "I don't think it's that bad. Don't worry, Grace. We'll whip this place into shape."

My brothers glanced at each other, giving subtle nods, as if acknowledging that I'd be fine. And that was true. Asher's brothers had always taken care of me. His whole family had.

"Who wants pizza?" I asked.

Hudson's hand shot into the air. "Me."

Madeline glanced at her cousin and giggled, then copied him. "Me."

"All right, Baileys, scoot," I said, trying to shoo Asher's brothers out the door. "You can come with us to pizza, but I don't think any of us wants to hang out here in all the dust anymore."

"That's fine, Grace," Evan said. He was the second oldest, and also tallest, at six-foot-four. "We're on our way to Gram's anyway."

"But, pizza," Gavin said. He was the baby of the family.

"Later, Gav," Logan said, slipping on a pair of sunglasses. "Grace, we'll see you later. Miles fam, nice to see you."

The Baileys said goodbye, then went out and piled into Logan's muscle car. It ran some of the time, so he loved driving it when it did. The engine started with a loud rumble as the rest of us made our way outside.

I gave everyone the name of the pizza place and basic directions. My hometown wasn't very big, so I didn't think they'd have any trouble finding it. They all got in their cars while I locked up.

I had to jiggle the key again to get it to lock. With a deep breath, I touched my fingertips to the door. One step closer.

The house we'd dreamed of was mine, and when Asher got home, it would be ours. I'd waited six years. Only two left.

I'd survived this long without him. I could wait a little longer.

GRACE AND ASHER'S story concludes in **Fighting for Us.**

DEAR READER

Dear Reader,

I know. I just did that thing. The dreaded cliffhanger. I'll address that. But first, I need to tell you a little story.

I've had Asher and Grace, and all the Baileys, in my head and heart for the last three years. I created a rough outline for the series, and even wrote an early draft of Grace and Asher's book, back in 2017. This was before I'd written the Miles Family, before Bootleg Springs... even before His Heart and Finding Ivy.

My plan for the series did not include this origin story. Grace and Asher's book was supposed to begin after Asher's prison sentence is over.

For various reasons, the series was temporarily shelved. I went on to write other things, including a little book called Broken Miles. Toward the end of that book, I realized something big.

Grace was a Miles.

In fact, Grace's father was Lawrence Miles. THAT was the secret he'd been hiding. One of them, at least. And that was the missing piece in Grace's backstory that I'd needed to know to really do justice to her character.

When I realized that, so many things changed.

Grace became an important side character in the Miles family series. The sibling they never knew. And there she was, wearing an engagement ring, yet never really mentioning who had given it to her.

When the time came to start writing this series, my plan was to rewrite that early draft of Asher and Grace's book. But then my assistant, Nikki, did a thing she does sometimes. She put an idea in my head. And I couldn't get it out.

What if I wrote the before? What if we got to experience the beginning of Asher and Grace's relationship? What if we could get to know them before he goes to prison?

It meant changing some things around in my editorial calendar, and essentially making room for an "extra" book. But man, was it worth it.

I learned things about these characters that I never would have known if I hadn't written this book. The deeper I got into writing it, the more I realized Nikki is basically a genius, and this part of their story HAD to be told. And not as backstory.

We all needed to be there when they fall in love. To walk with them as their childhood friendship blossoms into young love. Feel the things they feel, right there, up close and personal.

There was literally no other way to tell their story.

So I did it. I wrote what was going to be a medium length novella that turned essentially into a short novel.

And yes, it ends with a cliffhanger.

And yes, I know that's going to make some people mad.

I'm okay with it.

I'd argue it's not a TOTAL cliffhanger. It has an ending.

It's just not THE ending. And hopefully you went into this book knowing what you were getting into.

One of my early readers put it best. This isn't their happily ever after, but it is a **hopeful ever after**. This piece of their story ends on a sad note, but also one of hope. This is not the end for Asher and Grace.

In fact, their story is just beginning.

Love,
    CK

ACKNOWLEDGMENTS

Writing is often solitary, but there are so many wonderful people I rely on to help me along the way.

To my readers Michelle L., Robin C., Shannon M., Michelle R., Sandy W., Rebecca A., Jill G., thank you for helping with much needed research and answering so many of my questions!

To Alex, Jessica, and Nikki, thank you for your thorough beta read, and for holding my hand along the way.

To Erma, thank you for your time in proofreading and making sure we catch those last minute typos.

To Elayne, for cleaning up my words without sacrificing my voice, every single time. Also for your funny comments. Never stop doing that.

Another big thank you to Nikki for being my right hand and for loving these characters as much as I do.

And thank you to David and my kids for having my back and always believing in me.

ALSO BY CLAIRE KINGSLEY

For a full and up-to-date listing of Claire Kingsley books visit
www.clairekingsleybooks.com/books/

For comprehensive reading order, visit www.
clairekingsleybooks.com/reading-order/

The Bailey Brothers

Steamy, small-town family series. Five unruly brothers. Epic
pranks. A quirky, feuding town. Big HEAs. (Best read in order)

Protecting You (Asher and Grace part 1)

Fighting for Us (Asher and Grace part 2)

Unraveling Him (Evan and Fiona)

Rushing In (Gavin and Skylar)

Chasing Her Fire (Logan and Cara)

Rewriting the Stars (Levi and Annika)

The Miles Family

Sexy, sweet, funny, and heartfelt family series. Messy family. Epic
bromance. Super romantic. (Best read in order)

Broken Miles (Roland and Zoe)

Forbidden Miles (Brynn and Chase)

Reckless Miles (Cooper and Amelia)

Hidden Miles (Leo and Hannah)

Gaining Miles: A Miles Family Novella (Ben and Shannon)

~

Dirty Martini Running Club

Sexy, fun stand-alone romantic comedies with huge... hearts.

Everly Dalton's Dating Disasters (Everly, Hazel, and Nora)

Faking Ms. Right (Everly and Shepherd)

Falling for My Enemy (Hazel and Corban)

Marrying Mr. Wrong (Sophie and Cox)

(Nora's book coming soon)

~

Bluewater Billionaires

Hot, stand-alone romantic comedies. Lady billionaire BFFs and the badass heroes who love them.

The Mogul and the Muscle (Cameron and Jude)

The Price of Scandal, Wild Open Hearts, and Crazy for Loving You

More Bluewater Billionaire shared-world stand-alone romantic comedies by Lucy Score, Kathryn Nolan, and Pippa Grant

~

Bootleg Springs

by Claire Kingsley and Lucy Score

Hot and hilarious small-town romcom series with a dash of mystery and suspense. (Best read in order)

Whiskey Chaser (Scarlett and Devlin)

Sidecar Crush (Jameson and Leah Mae)

Moonshine Kiss (Bowie and Cassidy)

Bourbon Bliss (June and George)

Gin Fling (Jonah and Shelby)

Highball Rush (Gibson and I can't tell you)

Book Boyfriends

Hot, stand-alone romcoms that will make you laugh and make you swoon.

Book Boyfriend (Alex and Mia)

Cocky Roommate (Weston and Kendra)

Hot Single Dad (Caleb and Linnea)

Finding Ivy (William and Ivy)

A unique contemporary romance with a hint of mystery.

His Heart (Sebastian and Brooke)

A poignant and emotionally intense story about grief, loss, and the transcendent power of love.

The Always Series

Smoking hot, dirty talking bad boys with some angsty intensity.

Always Have (Braxton and Kylie)

Always Will (Selene and Ronan)

Always Ever After (Braxton and Kylie)

~

The Jetty Beach Series

Sexy small-town romance series with swoony heroes, romantic HEAs, and lots of big feels.

Behind His Eyes (Ryan and Nicole)

One Crazy Week (Melissa and Jackson)

Messy Perfect Love (Cody and Clover)

Operation Get Her Back (Hunter and Emma)

Weekend Fling (Finn and Juliet)

Good Girl Next Door (Lucas and Becca)

The Path to You (Gabriel and Sadie)

ABOUT THE AUTHOR

Claire Kingsley is a #1 Amazon bestselling author of sexy, heartfelt contemporary romance and romantic comedies. She writes sassy, quirky heroines, swoony heroes who love their women hard, panty-melting sexytimes, romantic happily ever afters, and all the big feels.

She can't imagine life without coffee, her Kindle, and the sexy heroes who inhabit her imagination. She lives in the inland Pacific Northwest with her three kids.

www.clairekingsleybooks.com